GAMER SQUAD

2

Close Encounters
of the Nerd Kind

GAMER SQUAD 2

Close Encounters of the Nerd Kind

KIM HARRINGTON

STERLING CHILDREN'S BOOKS
New York

STERLING CHILDREN'S BOOKS
New York

An Imprint of Sterling Publishing Co., Inc.
1166 Avenue of the Americas
New York, NY 10036

ISBN 978-1-4549-2613-9

Distributed in Canada by Sterling Publishing Co., Inc.
c/o Canadian Manda Group, 664 Annette Street
Toronto, Ontario, Canada M6S 2C8
Distributed in the United Kingdom by GMC Distribution Services
Castle Place, 166 High Street, Lewes, East Sussex, England BN7 1XU
Distributed in Australia by NewSouth Books
45 Beach Street, Coogee, NSW 2034, Australia

For information about custom editions, special sales, and premium
and corporate purchases, please contact Sterling Special Sales at
800-805-5489 or specialsales@sterlingpublishing.com.

Manufactured in Canada

Lot #:
2 4 6 8 10 9 7 5 3 1
06/17

sterlingpublishing.com

Design by Ryan Thomann

1

was going to be late for school if I didn't leave soon, but I couldn't move from my spot. The alien invasion had begun. I watched through my phone's screen as UFOs drifted down from the blue morning sky onto my front yard below.

I banged my finger against the screen, firing lasers at every enemy spaceship until they were all gone, and the words **YOU SAVED THE EARTH** flashed on the screen. Smiling broadly, I looked up to high-five my best friend, Charlie Tepper, but he wasn't there.

"Hey, Bex, did you win?" he called from his front yard next door.

At some point, he'd stopped playing and had wandered over to toss a football with his older brother, Jason. That was a sight I'd never get used to. Until recently, Jason's only contact with his brother was to bully and insult him. But after we nearly lost Charlie in an, um, monster incident, Jason had been nicer. And it helped that, once he actually began spending quality time with Charlie, Jason realized that his nerdy little brother had a secret. Surprisingly, Charlie had quite an arm on him. So Jason had made it his life's mission to teach Charlie everything he could about football. I didn't think Charlie would be interested for longer than a day. But it had lasted the rest of the summer, and he'd even joined the middle school football team. Though I still clung to the hope that the whole thing would be a passing fad.

"Of course I won," I said as I strolled over to them.

It wasn't as conceited as it sounded. I'd be the first to admit the things I was bad at (which were many). But gaming wasn't one of them. I was an awesome gamer, and I'd even started to teach myself how to code using online apps. It came easy to me, like science did to Charlie. Though he spent less time doing chemistry experiments in his basement these days.

"Heads up!" Jason yelled.

I ducked just in time to avoid getting a football lodged in my nostril.

"We should go," Charlie said. "See you later, Jason."

Jason was a freshman and thankfully the high school was in the opposite direction. I liked walking to middle school with Charlie alone. Lately it seemed like the only time we got to really talk. We only shared one class together—science. And lunch was so crowded that sometimes in all of the chaos, we didn't end up at the same table.

Things had been so much simpler in elementary school.

"So what did you think of that science homework?" I asked, hefting my backpack higher on my shoulder.

"It was pretty easy." Charlie kicked at a pebble and it flew a few feet in front of us. "The field trip tomorrow night sounds awesome."

"Yeah, it does." I kicked the pebble farther. This was a game we played most mornings. We'd find a pebble and take turns kicking it all the way to school.

He took a turn, launching the pebble ten feet down the sidewalk. "You're really into *Alien Invasion*, huh? Do you think it's as good as *Monsters Unleashed*?"

The makers of *Alien Invasion*, Veratrum Games, had previously created a game called *Monsters Unleashed*. We'd been totally obsessed with it over the summer. Until some of the video game monsters got *really* unleashed and we had to save the town from real live snarling beasts.

"It's not quite as good, but it feels safer." I laughed, and he joined in.

Both of us had vowed never to play *Monsters Unleashed* again. But I was happy when *Alien Invasion* came out. It was another augmented reality game, which meant that when you were playing, it looked like the game was taking place in the real world. It used the phone's camera and graphics card to do the trick. And there was nothing like battling video game aliens in your school parking lot.

Even our science teacher, Mr. Durr, liked the game. If you played at night, there was a really cool extra feature that "was actually educational," he said. When you held the phone up to the sky, a star map filled in, showing exactly what stars and planets you were looking at. I'd learned a lot about astronomy while I protected our planet from fake aliens.

"You still haven't played at night yet," I pointed out.

Charlie's parents had finally agreed to get him a cell phone after he'd joined the football team, so that he could text them when it was time to pick him up from practice. When we used to play mobile games together, he always had to borrow his mother's phone. It was great that he now had his own—if he ever had free time to use it.

"I've heard the game's ten times cooler at night," Charlie said.

My face lit up as I thought of an idea. "How about tonight? Eight p.m. My backyard. The weather app this morning said it was going to be clear skies. Perfect for playing!"

Charlie held the school's front door open for me. "I can't. I have football practice after school. And then I'm going out for ice cream with the team. And then I'll have to do all my homework."

My heart sank into my gray Converse sneakers. I followed him into the school, feeling like I was losing my best friend. We'd been inseparable since I'd moved in next door when we were five. We didn't even mind when other kids teased us about being boy/girl best friends. But since we started middle school three weeks ago, things felt like they were changing. Or, more specifically, Charlie was changing.

"Hey, do you have any new science jokes?" I asked. "You haven't told me one in a while."

Charlie raised his eyebrows. "You hate my science jokes."

"I don't *hate* them."

He gave me a look.

"Okay, I used to think they were a little annoying," I admitted. "But, strangely, I miss them."

His science jokes were totally dorky, and he sometimes came out with them at inappropriate times. But everything was suddenly moving too fast. I just wanted one thing to stay the same.

"Well, I can't think of any right now," he said with a shrug.

Then the bell rang so loudly it made my ears ache.

"Gotta go!" Charlie called.

Kids darted left and right, squealing with their friends. I shuffled toward my classroom, head down, feeling like a lost puppy. Then I felt a shove, like someone had pushed my backpack. I looked around, but the hall was chaos. It was probably an accident, some kid bumping me while trying to squeeze by.

I settled into my seat in English class and put my backpack on the floor. But then I noticed something. A white piece of paper had been shoved into the side pocket. I glanced around. No one was paying any attention to me, as usual. So I slipped the note out and unfolded it. When I saw what it said, my heart did a cartwheel.

YOU'RE INVITED
TO JOIN TGS. TONIGHT,
THE COMMON, 7 P.M.

What was this? A secret group? I had no idea. But I couldn't wait to find out.

2

School passed in a blur, and I sped through my homework all afternoon. I couldn't wait until seven. I was so excited to find out what TGS was. It was definitely taking my mind off the way things were with Charlie.

I slid into my seat at the dinner table as my father put out a platter of chicken and potatoes. My dad was an incredible cook. Even plain old chicken and potatoes tasted awesome. And he loved coming home from the office and slipping on his apron. He said cooking helped him "decompress." I didn't really understand, but his process ended with tasty noms, so that's all the mattered.

Mom settled onto the seat beside me, typing wildly on her phone.

"A phone at the table?" my dad said with a wink. "Really?"

Mom chuckled but continued typing. "One second. I just have to finish this last email."

The "no phones at the table" rule had been created for me, so that I'd stop gaming long enough to put food in my mouth. But now that the personalized jewelry business Mom had started out of her home office had taken off, she broke the rule more than anyone.

"Okay, I'm done!" she announced and pushed the phone away.

I stabbed a roasted potato with my fork and blew on it until it cooled. "How was work?"

Mom let out a breath that made her bangs flutter. "Busy."

"My day was nonstop meetings," Dad said with a sigh. "But I'm home and decompressed! How was school?"

See? He really liked that word. I held up a finger as I chewed through a bite. "Pretty good. I'm excited about the field trip to the observatory tomorrow night."

"That sounds wonderful," Dad said. "Is Charlie excited, too? I know he's always been into the sciences."

At the mention of Charlie, I felt my shoulders sag a bit. My parents knew that he'd joined the football team, and I was sure they'd noticed we were spending less time together. But I tried not to show how much it was bothering me.

"Yeah," I said, my voice cracking. "I think he's excited."

My parents shared a look.

"We've been thinking," Mom said carefully. "Maybe you need to . . . widen your circle of friends."

I could tell by the way they tiptoed around the conversation that this was something they'd discussed ahead of time. Something they were worried about. I hated it when my parents worried about me. I mean, I knew it was their job and all, but I was fine. Everything was fine.

I cleared my throat. "That's a good idea. Actually, I'm meeting some kids from school at the common tonight after dinner."

"Great!" Mom said.

"Wonderful!" Dad echoed.

The rest of the dinner conversation spiraled into current events and politics, like it sometimes did. But I was glad the spotlight was off me. Having to talk to my parents about my social life was always so awkward.

I helped my mom with the dishes and grabbed a light jacket. September in Massachusetts was unpredictable. It could feel like summer one day and midwinter the next. I didn't know what to expect when I went to the common. And I wasn't just talking about the weather.

The walk was quick and uneventful, though strange. I hardly ever walked downtown without Charlie. Wolcott Common was an open, grassy area where kids played and people had picnics and stuff. There were always at least a handful of people milling about. So I was surprised when I got there and found . . . no one.

I glanced at my phone. It was seven o'clock. I wasn't late. Was the note a trick of some kind? Did the TGS people change their mind, whoever they were?

"*Psst . . .*"

The sound came from the pretty white gazebo. I squinted and could make out someone's shadow.

As I walked toward it, my nerves prickled. Maybe it wasn't such a great idea to go meet a stranger, even in a public place.

But when I got closer, I realized the sound wasn't coming from a stranger after all. And then I got even more nervous.

Marcus Moore stood in the center of the gazebo, hands in the pockets of his jeans, looking super cool in his black Veratrum Games T-shirt. I'd had a crush on Marcus since, well, since I knew how to have crushes. He was one grade ahead of me, wicked smart, and the best gamer I knew. Of course, along with those skills came an unfortunately large ego. And the fact that he didn't care what anyone thought of him was both adorable and horrible because he could be annoyingly sarcastic at times.

"Is this . . . the TGS meeting?" I asked.

"No. It's a sewing circle."

Like now. This was one of those times.

I rolled my eyes. "If you're going to be a jerk, I'll just leave."

He quickly descended the steps of the gazebo to the grass. "Come on. I was just joking. You're so serious, Bexley Grayson."

"It's Bex. You know that." He probably also knew that I hated my full name. And that was probably why he used it. But I wouldn't crack a smile or give him any sort of reaction. I stood, stone-faced.

"You're probably wondering what that note was all about," he said.

"Nah. I came here to look at the stars."

The side of his mouth lifted up. "Looks like two can play that game."

Dang it. I couldn't complain about him being sarcastically rude if my reaction was to do it right back. "So," I said, evening out my voice. "What does *TGS* stand for?"

"The Gamer Squad," he answered. "It's an invitation-only, elite group of the top gamers in town. And after how you handled the *Monsters Unleashed* debacle, we think you're the perfect fit."

My eyes widened. Was this heaven? Had I died and gone to a perfect place?

"Th-that sounds incredible," I stammered. "What do you do?"

"Well, we're relatively new. But we game together, obviously. We try out betas. Play around with some coding so we can build our own apps."

I had to stop myself from clapping with excitement. "That sounds awesome. We're in. We're totally in!"

Marcus raised an eyebrow. "We?"

"Charlie and I." I almost added a *duh* because it should have been obvious.

Marcus's expression turned serious. "The invitation was only for you."

All of that excitement drained out of me like a dead battery. I couldn't join a gamer group without Charlie. We were gaming partners. Even now, when he was busy with his new hobby, I couldn't imagine heading off to secret gamer meetings without him. Would I have to lie about where I was going? If the group found an awesome new game, would I have to play it without him? All summer I'd been worried that middle school would tear our friendship apart. Whether that happened or not, it certainly wasn't going to be my doing.

"I'm out, then," I said sadly.

Marcus's mouth dropped open. "You're rejecting me? I mean, us?"

I shrugged. "I can't join without Charlie. He's my best friend."

Marcus snapped his jaw shut and his eyes flared.

"Have fun playing games by yourself, then. Because your supposed best friend has already moved on."

He stormed off in a huff. I couldn't believe he'd gotten so upset. I wasn't rejecting him personally; I just couldn't join his group if they weren't also inviting Charlie. It wasn't the right thing to do. Marcus should understand that. He knew what Charlie and I had been through last summer with the monsters.

As I turned to watch him march away, I saw what he'd meant when he said Charlie "had moved on." A bunch of kids, including my best friend, ambled down the sidewalk past the common in their football gear. Practice had ended and they were walking to the Ice Cream Shack. It wasn't a surprise, really. Charlie had told me about it. That was why he couldn't play *Alien Invasion* with me tonight.

It hadn't bothered me too much at the time. But watching him now with his new buddies, laughing and shoving one another while I stood in the darkened common alone . . .

I couldn't help but wonder if Marcus was right.

3

The bus was packed. My stomach tightened as I glanced at all the rows of seats. I'd been so excited all day about the field trip that night. But I'd totally forgotten we'd have to take a school bus to get there. Buses gave me anxiety. Trying to find a seat, fear of being rejected, feeling the pressure of sticking to the rules of bus placement (nerds in the front, troublemakers and cool kids in the back). It made me glad Charlie and I lived close enough to walk to school every day.

I spied Charlie alone in a seat halfway down. His face lit up, and he gave me a wave. Immediately, my anxiety released, and I exhaled a deep breath.

But then, before I could reach Charlie, Robbie Martinez sat down next to him. Robbie was another seventh grader on the football team. He seemed nice, and Charlie had been talking about him a lot lately. But that was my seat! I looked at Charlie, waiting for him to tell Robbie that the seat was taken. But he didn't even glance at me. He stared, with rapt attention, as Robbie told some story from gym glass.

I felt a shove in the center of my back.

"Come on!" someone yelled. "Move!"

My heart sped up as I slowly made my way down the aisle, frantically looking for somewhere to sit. None of my other friends were on this field trip—only Charlie. Each seat was either already taken with two people or one person and the universal sign for "don't even try it," a hand or backpack saving the second spot. As far as I could see, it was rejection after rejection. What would I do? Push a kid's hand away and insist that I sit? Grab a spot on the floor? Just keep on going right out the back emergency exit door?

"Excuse me," a girl said, squeezing past. I didn't have to look to know who it was. I recognized the voice of Willa Tanaka, my friend, then enemy, then maybe friend, but we hadn't really figured it out yet. If you're confused, don't worry. So was I.

Willa pushed by me to sit with Chloe Forte, who had been saving her a spot. But then another girl who'd also been saving a spot for Willa got mad and insisted on pushing into the same seat, squishing three in a row. The good news was she'd left a completely empty seat. I launched myself into it like it was the last lifeboat on a sinking ship. Then I leaned my head back against the seat and closed my eyes.

I couldn't believe Charlie had dumped me for Robbie. Was he really changing? Was he leaving me behind? My phone buzzed in my pocket, and I pulled it out to read the new text.

Charlie: I'm so sorry. He just sat down and started talking, and I didn't have the heart to kick him out. Forgive me?

I chewed on my lower lip. Of course, the whole thing was because Charlie was so nice. He hadn't abandoned me on purpose. I shouldn't have thought that, even for a second. I typed back a quick message:

Totally! No problem!

Now I only had to stew in the embarrassment of being the one student in a single seat. Some kids had even gone three together. I swallowed hard and looked out the window. The bus started rolling forward.

My seat shook as someone plunked down next to me. I turned and my mouth opened in surprise.

Willa flipped her long, shiny black hair over one shoulder. "I wasn't going to stay squished three to a seat this whole ride. That's ridiculous."

I glanced over at the two girls she'd left behind, who were both pouting and glaring at me as if I'd somehow stolen Willa. In fact, Willa and I had been friends when we were little. As we got older, she got prettier and I got nerdier, and then she dumped me for the mean-girl crew. In order to remake her image as a popular girl, she'd pushed me away. But then she helped Charlie and me rid the town of the monsters that showed up this summer, and that had brought her meanness down from a ten to, like, a five.

"I'm not in the mood to talk, though," she said, popping in a pair of earbuds.

Okay, maybe a seven.

What I'd learned long ago when we became friends, though, was that Willa wasn't as mean as she sometimes sounded, she was just *really* blunt. Like, you wouldn't ask her if she liked your new haircut unless you wanted the honest truth. But she was also smart and hilarious and had a sixth sense for fashion and style. I missed her friendship after she'd left me behind, and we were starting to get that back. But I wasn't ready to trust her quite yet.

Before I knew it, the bus slowed to a stop and I could see the huge white building with the observatory dome on top. My leg started bouncing up and down in my seat. Mr. Durr stood at the front of the bus to give us one last lecture about "appropriate field trip behavior" and "school expectations," and then we were off.

Even the lobby of the observatory building was cool. We pushed past the front desk, where a young guy looked completely overwhelmed by the crowd of seventh graders pouring in. Glass cases lined the walls, full of NASA memorabilia—dehydrated astronaut food packets, mission patches, and pins. They even had an actual tire from a Space Shuttle *Discovery* flying mission. I was so enthralled that I'd almost forgotten I was with other people until I felt a hand on my shoulder.

"Bex," Charlie said. "This way."

I followed Charlie to a corner on the opposite side of the room where an actual meteorite was mounted that you were allowed to touch. I waited my turn and then slid my finger along the smooth, dark rock. This thing had traveled millions of miles through space and burned through our atmosphere to land on Earth. That was quite a trip. Maybe even worse than taking a school bus.

"Check it out," Charlie said, pulling me toward another corner. He was like a kid on Christmas morning, except all of the presents were unwrapped and were totally nerdy. "This scale tells you what you'd weigh on other planets."

"Let's see what I would weigh on Mars," I said, stepping on the platform.

Charlie pressed a couple buttons and selected Mars. "On Mars, where there's less gravity than on Earth, you would weigh thirty-four pounds." He pressed a different button. "But on Jupiter? Two hundred, twelve pounds."

I chuckled. "This place is so cool."

Mr. Durr clapped from the center of the room to get our attention. "Okay, kids. Time to line up to take turns looking through the telescope. Remember, I expect your best behavior. Dr. Maria McCafferty, the observatory's astronomer, will take it from here."

A tall, thin woman with long blonde hair stepped up next to our teacher. "You can call me Dr. Maria. Tonight, we'll be looking at three space objects. We'll look at the moon last because it's so bright that your eyes will take a while to adjust afterward. First, we'll gaze at the Ring Nebula. Can anyone tell me what a nebula is?"

Charlie's hand shot up into the air. "A cloud of gas and dust."

"Correct," Dr. Maria said with a smile. "The Ring Nebula was formed from a dying star. It's two thousand light-years away, but you're each going to get a chance to see it now."

Charlie's face looked like he'd just won the lottery.

But his excitement waned twenty minutes later when we were still in line and hadn't yet had our turn. The line snaked up a curved, narrow staircase to the observation area where the giant telescope stood waiting. The dome of the observatory was open, and I rubbed my arms against the chill in the air. The sky looked different up here. It went on and on, like a never-ending display of twinkling lights.

It gave me an idea.

I pulled my phone out of my pocket and held it up to show Charlie. "I know what we can do to pass the time."

His eyes lit up. "Great idea! I still haven't played at night yet. This is going to be cool."

We opened the *Alien Invasion* game on both of our phones and chose Nighttime Mode. I held my phone up to the sky and the star map filled in what I was seeing. Mars hung low in the sky, rusty red. The angled *W* of Cassiopeia glowed brightly.

"So cool," Charlie said. "Why haven't I made time to do this yet?"

"Well, you've been busy." I tried to make it sound like a fact and not me whining.

He grinned. "Should we summon the aliens?"

I grinned right back. "Let's do it."

I pressed the Summon button, and moments later the screen filled up with alien spaceships of all kinds drifting from various corners of the galaxy. I used the precise laser on single ships and the mega-laser on groups of ships. You only got so many tries with the mega-laser, so you had to use it only when you really needed it. But I'd figured all of this out the first day I'd had the game. By now, it was automatic.

The sky was cleared of any threats in less than ninety seconds, my new record. The screen lit up with the message, **YOU SAVED THE EARTH.** Charlie still wasn't done, so I gave him some tips as he finished the mission.

Then it was our turn at the telescope. Perfect timing!

I took only about ten seconds because I didn't want to make all the kids behind me wait too long. The Ring Nebula looked like a bluish-gray doughnut in space, but it was pretty cool to think about how far away it was and that an exploding or dying star had caused it.

When all the kids had seen it, Dr. Maria took a moment to tell us what we would be looking at next. "So, who wants to see a star?" she called out.

All the kids whooped and clapped.

"Vega is a blue-white star. It's the fifth-brightest star in our sky. And, as far as star distances go, it's pretty close. Only twenty-five light-years away. Do you know what that means?"

Again, Charlie's hand shot up. "If we could move at the speed of light, which we currently can't, it would still take twenty-five years to get there."

"Correct again." Dr. Maria gave him a "teacher's favorite" smile. Though in this case, it would be an astronomer's favorite. "The light from Vega that we're going to see right now left the star twenty-five years ago."

A chorus of "wows" came from the crowd as we shuffled back into a line.

Charlie was super-pumped again. Unfortunately, the line moved super slowly again. Dr. Maria did her best to chat with the kids who were waiting, though, to make the time seem to go by faster. Charlie examined all the machines and monitors along the way. When it was almost our turn, he cocked his head at an interesting-looking one near the telescope. The machine had no top on it, just a bunch of exposed wires.

"What's the machine with all the wires?" he asked Dr. Maria as she walked by.

She waved her hand dismissively. "Oh, nothing yet."

"What *will* it be?"

"Well, if I can get it to work . . . " She paused like she was trying to figure out a way to explain it. "Some equipment is to detect life in the universe. To search. To listen." Then she pointed to the machine. "This one is to talk."

Charlie rubbed his chin. "So this device is to signal in case someone is searching for us."

"Exactly!" She smiled, genuinely pleased with Charlie's interest. Then her smile fell. "But, like I said, it's a work in progress. And many of my colleagues think we should stay quiet and not let extraterrestrials know we're here."

"Why?" I asked.

"So they don't invade us," Willa said from behind me. "Haven't you seen any sci-fi movies?"

Charlie spoke up again, "It's like that famous Stephen Hawking quote. 'If aliens visit us, the outcome would be much as when Columbus landed in America, which didn't turn out well for the Native Americans.'"

Impressed again, Dr. Maria's eyebrows rose. "Food for thought, young man. But right now, it's your turn."

While Charlie tiptoed up to the eyepiece of the giant telescope, I launched *Alien Invasion* again. I selected Nighttime Mode and looked around with the star map. I'd wait to hit the Summon button until after my turn at the telescope.

The kids behind me were getting restless, their voices getting louder the longer they had to wait. But that didn't matter to me, because Charlie had finished and finally it was my turn.

I leaned my face up to the eyepiece, blinked quickly, and then focused my sight. Vega was a beautiful, bright blue. Other kids had described it as twinkling, but to me it seemed like the star shimmered.

"Come on!" a voice from the back cried. "Hurry up!"

I'd had only a few seconds with it. But everyone was getting bored and sick of waiting, and that only brought trouble. So I finished up and stepped to the side, near Dr. Maria's half-constructed machine.

A jostling started near the back of the line.

"Hey, no pushing!" someone yelled.

But, of course, someone else pushed in response. One kid fell, and, because they were packed in so tightly, the rest toppled over like tumbling dominoes. I had my phone in my hand, and when someone slammed into me, I accidentally hit the Summon button as I went down. My head bonked off the side of the giant telescope and my phone flew onto Dr. Maria's mystery machine.

Great. The invasion was going to start, but I wouldn't be able to shoot down the aliens because I wasn't ready. By the time I righted myself and plucked my phone from between two wires, forty-five seconds had passed with zero aliens lasered. This was going to hurt my speed and accuracy averages.

I groaned and left the telescope platform. The lobby was much more appealing right now. There was actually room to breathe. My head throbbed where I'd hit it against the telescope. And when I finally had a moment to focus on the game in my hand, I saw that I'd failed the mission. For the first time, the screen didn't give me the congratulatory message it usually did when a level ended.

This time, it said, **YOU DOOMED THE EARTH**.

4

The bus brought us back to the school parking lot. Charlie and I could have walked home; we lived close enough. But because it was late, our parents insisted on us getting a ride home. Charlie's mom was going to pass by on her way back from the late shift at the hospital, so she'd volunteered. But she was late.

I crossed my arms and exhaled loudly. "If we walked, we would've been home by now."

Charlie shook his head. "Parents. Always doing annoying stuff like making sure we're safe."

I gave him a look, and he gave me one right back.

"So what are you doing tomorrow?" he asked.

I rubbed the side of my head. It was a little tender, but no harm done. "Nothing. Why, do you want to hang out? We could play *Alien Invasion* at the park, fix my score averages."

"I have a football game," he said, shuffling from one foot to the other. "I was hoping you would come."

"Oh," I said, trying not to let the disappointment show in my voice. "Sure."

"It's just that . . . " he hesitated. "I'm a little nervous."

My heart clenched. "No reason to be nervous! I'll be there, waving like an idiot from the stands."

He smiled from ear to ear. "Thanks."

I shook my head in disbelief. "I still can't believe you're the quarterback."

"Backup quarterback."

"Still."

"I probably won't even play. I'll probably sit on the bench the whole game."

"Still! A few weeks ago you didn't even know how many points were in a touchdown, and now you're part of the team."

A bashful smile formed on his face. "Well, it turns out throwing the ball accurately is really just physics. You see the player who needs the ball and then it's a matter of what speed and degree to get it there. Plus, I'm great at memorizing the playbook."

I elbowed him in the side. "I'm so glad you're still a nerd."

He rolled his eyes. "Always."

"I'll be there tomorrow," I said.

His mom pulled up in her white SUV and rolled down the window. "I'm so sorry I'm late!"

"It's okay," Charlie said. "Only three people tried to kidnap us."

She laughed and waved to Mr. Durr, who was waiting by the now-empty school bus to make sure everyone got picked up okay. As we climbed into the backseat, Mrs. Tepper gave me a quick hello. She was still wearing her navy-blue scrubs.

Once the car started moving, Mrs. Tepper began her usual barrage of questions. "So how was it? Did you like the telescope? Was the astronomer nice? What did you see?"

Charlie ignored the first few questions and focused on the last one, describing the Ring Nebula and Vega. We never got to see the moon as planned because the class had failed the whole "good behavior" thing. Apparently, pushing and shoving gets you kicked out of an observatory.

The car pulled into the Teppers' driveway, and I hopped out. "Thanks for the ride!"

"See you tomorrow!" Charlie reminded me.

"I'll be the loudest fan in the bleachers," I lied. I'd go, of course. But, unless Charlie actually went in, I'd probably play games on my phone the whole time and clap when everyone else clapped.

Speaking of games, I probably had time for one last *Alien Invasion* level before going inside. It would be a shame to waste such a beautiful, clear night.

I wound around my house, passing the living room window, where a blue flickering light told me my parents were watching TV, and headed into the backyard. It was quiet and peaceful, with only the distant sound of a cricket chirping. Under the light of the half moon, I slid my phone out and opened the game.

Holding the phone up to the sky, I slowly turned in a circle, taking in all the star map had to offer. Constellations and stars were labeled. I even found Vega again. I'd never been as much of a science nerd as Charlie. I was more of a gamer geek. But tonight I understood his fascination.

Suddenly, I froze in place. I had the eerie sense that someone was watching me. I was facing the back of my house, phone held high. I quickly glanced at all the windows and didn't see anyone looking out. But I didn't expect to. It felt like someone was *behind* me.

Little hairs stood up on the back of my neck under my ponytail. *Stop it, Bex*, I said to myself. *You're being paranoid.* No one was outside, hanging around my backyard. And the woods lining the edge of our property weren't like real woods that stretched for distances and had actual, scary animals in them. The trees just gave the house some privacy from the street on the other side. There was nothing there.

But then I heard a noise, like a careful footstep on a crackly dead leaf.

Your mind is playing tricks on you, I thought. *Just turn and see that no one's there.* I spun around, expecting to see nothing. Or, at worst, Charlie trying to sneak up to scare me.

What I did not expect to see was an alien.

5

squeezed my eyes shut. Apparently I'd hit my head harder than I'd thought at the observatory. This was a hallucination. It had to be. I took a deep breath and reopened my eyes. But the alien was still there, looking at me like I was crazy. Or, at least, I thought it was an alien. It didn't look like any of the monsters I'd met this summer. It looked more like one of the alien species from *Alien Invasion*.

It had three legs, like a camera tripod, and a long, ribbed neck, on top of which sat a square head. Its eyes were on its neck. Above, on its face, were its mouth and a hole I assumed served as a nose. It had no hair anywhere, and its skin was pale blue and almost translucent. I could see veins and stuff underneath. The whole package was really gross, actually. It wasn't wearing any clothes but, thankfully, it had as much private business as a Ken doll. I really didn't need to see alien privates right now—I was traumatized enough as it was.

It took a step toward me, and I instinctively took a quick step back.

Then another creature emerged from the woods, breathing heavily, like it had jogged there and was out of shape. This alien looked different, more like me. It also had three legs—so weird—but its face stuff was all in the right, human order, and it had a bird's nest-looking thing on the top of its head that I assumed was badly styled hair.

The uglier alien looked at the new alien and even though its face was, like, upside down, I recognized the expression. Fear. Why was one alien afraid of the other one?

"Um, hi," I said, my voice trembling. "I'm Bex. I'm a human. I'm peaceful."

The way they stared reminded me of William Shakespaw, my neighbor's dog. Sometimes I'd chat him up, and he'd stare at my mouth, cocking his head to the side, like he was waiting to pick out any words he recognized.

Then one of the aliens responded. The uglier, upside-down faced one. It made a strange clicking sound with its mouth. Bad-hair alien responded with its own clicking sounds, though they were deeper and more ominous. Then Upside-Down Face increased its clicking and put its skinny arms on its sides. Oh, that one was upset. No doubt.

I wondered if they'd notice if I just slowly backed away while they argued about something in their own language. But after only two steps Bad Hair's head snapped toward my direction. Then it hissed.

This was not good.

It stepped closer to me, hands raised in the air, with claws where its fingernails should be. Every muscle in my body tightened in panic. Bad Hair snarled and clawed at the air between us. This was bad. Very, very bad. I got scratched by a cat once and had to get a tetanus shot. If this thing drew blood, who knew what kind of intergalactic disease I'd end up with.

Then I remembered that I'd saved myself from monsters using the *Monsters Unleashed* game over the summer. If these aliens had anything to do with *Alien Invasion*, maybe I could put them back where they came from by using the game. Simple!

I still had the phone in my trembling hands, though the app had closed. Heart racing, I opened it back up. Instead of pointing the phone toward the sky, I aimed it at Bad Hair in front of me. I centered the alien in my laser-sights and hit the Fire button. The game made its usual *beep-boop* sound effect, and I saw the laser like I always did on the screen, but nothing happened in the real world.

What the—? This worked with the monsters! I lined the alien up again, imagining that it was one of the hundreds of UFOs I'd shot down in the game, and frantically hit the button over and over. But Bad Hair didn't get zapped away in a ball of light. It didn't disappear from the real world and land back in my game.

It moved closer.

Its eyes flared underneath that messy mop of

hair, and its translucent skin glowed. I think I made it mad.

"Um, okay." I put my hands up in surrender. "I can see that we're having a miscommunication. I wasn't trying to harm you. I just had the dumb idea that I could send you back where you belong with my phone. I was trying to do you a favor. But now I see that I was wrong."

My words didn't seem to calm it at all. In fact, it took a large, terrifying step closer.

Upside-down Face, however, seemed more chill. That alien was looking at me with a new expression on its face. I didn't know what any of it meant, though. I didn't know why two aliens showed up in my backyard. I didn't know why one seemed intent on eating me (or whatever it had planned—definitely nothing good). I didn't know why the one that was scarier-looking seemed nicer. All I knew was that standing there in terror wasn't helping me at all.

I aimed a thumb at my house. "Okay, this has been a good talk. But I'm going to go now."

Taking a chance, I turned around and started speed-walking toward the back door. I figured running was a bad idea. Some animals had prey instincts that automatically kicked in when they saw something run. I'd seen it myself with William Shakespaw and an unfortunate squirrel. But speed-walking was fine, right? *No reason to chase me, Mr. Alien. Nothing to see here. I'm just escaping is all.*

The alien roared and charged toward me.

Uh-oh. Speed-walk plan failure. Time for Plan B: straight-up running.

Even at my fastest speed, Bad Hair was faster. My heart pumped wildly. I felt like one of those gazelles you see on animal shows, with the lion charging toward it. I risked a glance over my shoulder. It was catching up. I was done for!

And then, like a WWE wrestler, Upside-down Face came flying out of nowhere and dropped an alien elbow into Bad Hair's face. I gasped as the two aliens fell to the ground, rolling and fighting. Actually I would have loved to stick around and watch,. How often do you get to see an alien brawl? But midfight, Upside-down Face spoke to me. In *my* language. It was only two words, but they were all I needed to hear.

It said, "Get away!"

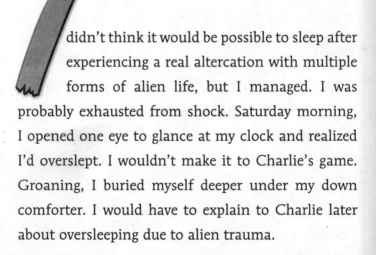

didn't think it would be possible to sleep after experiencing a real altercation with multiple forms of alien life, but I managed. I was probably exhausted from shock. Saturday morning, I opened one eye to glance at my clock and realized I'd overslept. I wouldn't make it to Charlie's game. Groaning, I buried myself deeper under my down comforter. I would have to explain to Charlie later about oversleeping due to alien trauma.

Eyes closed and slipping in and out of sleep, I reran the previous night's events through my mind. Real aliens showed up in my backyard. One of them seemed curious, and the other, just plain mean. Upside-down Face saved my life and told me to get away. And after I'd escaped to safety and risked looking out the window to check on the alien fight, they were gone. Maybe if I stayed in bed under this warm blanket all day, I could convince myself it had all been a dream.

Someone nudged my foot, which hung over the side of the bed.

I rolled over, groaning. "Five more minutes."

I didn't want to get up, because then I'd wake completely and have to somehow deal with what happened. The person nudged me again, harder. It was strange. Mom usually woke me with a kiss on the forehead, and Dad with his general loudness and clomping footsteps. I opened my eyes and peered over my shoulder.

The alien from last night—Upside-down Face—stood by the side of my bed.

I shot up and jumped off the bed, taking a tangle of blankets and sheets with me. The alien was blocking the path to the door, so I dashed to the opposite corner.

Okay, I was definitely all the way awake now.

This was the nice alien who'd saved me, but I still didn't like the fact that it was hanging out in my room, waking me up.

"Wh-what do you want?" I stammered.

The alien made its strange clicking sounds again, but softly, like it didn't want to attract attention from anyone else in the house.

"I don't understand," I said. "You spoke to me in English last night." Well, two words, but still. "Can you do that again?"

The alien turned its blockhead back and forth, like it was looking for something in my room. Then it held a hand out and pretended to press buttons on its hand with its finger. I couldn't believe an alien had traveled all the way to Earth just to play charades with me, but I'd roll with it.

"Buttons! Tapping! Morse code?"

The alien let out a burst of air that seemed sort of like a sigh and dropped its upside down face into its hands.

Then something clicked in my brain. Could it

mean my phone? I'd had my phone in bed with me last night. It had to be in this pile of bedding on the floor. I held up one finger, which I'd hoped was a universally-known sign for "hold on a second." Then I tore through the pile of sheets on the floor.

"Found it!" I called, holding the phone in the air.

The alien enthusiastically bowed its head. So I'd done something right. But now what? I thought through the events of last night. I had my phone with me in the backyard. The *Alien Invasion* game was off when the aliens did their angry click-talking. But then I'd reopened it to try to laser Bad Hair back to its home planet. And after that, Upside-Down Face seemed to understand me and had even told me to get away.

My eyes widened. Did the game work as a translator app?

I excitedly tapped on the icon and waited for the game to open. Then I spoke. "Can you understand me now?"

"Yes, thank you," the alien said. Its mouth moved the same way as before, but its strange clicking sounds were now words. Robotic-sounding words that came from my phone's speaker. I hadn't even noticed last night that when the alien said, "get away," the sound had come from the phone in my hand.

But now . . . this was amazing. The *Alien Invasion* game was working as an actual alien translator. I was probably about to have the first human–alien conversation in the history of time! What would its first question about Earth be? Adrenaline shot through me. I couldn't take the suspense!

A knock came on my bedroom door. "Bexley? Are you awake?"

My mother. My eyes nearly popped out of my head. And the alien's eyes did, too. Except, you know, they were on its neck.

"Um, yeah, I'm awake but, uh,"—fake cough, fake cough—"I'm not feeling super-great. I'm going to keep resting my eyes."

"You didn't come down for breakfast. You must be starving."

Mom labored under the delusion that if I skipped one meal I would immediately drop dead. And then everyone would say it was her fault and call her a bad mother because I didn't eat a bowl of cereal.

"I'm fine," I called. "Not hungry at all."

"Okay," she said in her *I'm clearly concerned* voice. "I'll check back on you later. Get some rest."

I waited until her footsteps echoed back down the stairs. Then I turned to the alien. "We can talk now. What would you like to know?"

The alien cleared its wrinkled throat. "Are you the leader of this world?"

I blinked. "Um, what?"

The alien pointed to the phone in my hand. "Is it not working correctly?"

"No, it's working. I just—why would you think I'm the leader of Earth?"

"Because you were the one who summoned us."

7

y head spun like a bad carnival ride.

I summoned aliens to Earth?

"How? What? Why do you think that?" I asked, fumbling for the right words.

The alien pointed a long finger at my phone. "That is your device, correct?"

"Yes, it's my cell phone."

"That device summoned us. And since it is your device, therefore, you summoned us."

Okay, solid logic. "I didn't mean to summon anyone. I play a game called *Alien Invasion,* but it's just a game . . . " Until it landed in an astronomer's mystery machine right as I'd pressed the Summon button.

I hung my head. *Oh, no. I'd done it again.*

But I had no time for self-pity. I had to get some answers before my mom came back. "Where are you from?"

The alien aimed a finger at the sky. "A planet that orbits the star you call Vega."

That's what the equipment was pointed at last night. It all made sense.

"Are you a boy or a girl?" I asked.

"Things aren't that simple. But for your purposes, you can call me a woman."

Okay, so she was a grown-up. I couldn't really tell because she was four feet tall and—though she had more wrinkles than a Shar-Pei—that could've been their norm.

"My name is Bexley, but my friends call me Bex."

"What should I call you?" the alien asked.

"Bex," I said. "And what's your name?"

"It does not translate."

"Okay, then please say it yourself in your natural language."

The alien's mouth released a bunch of clicks and high-pitched whistles, kind of like dolphin talk.

I shook my head. "Yeah, that's not going to work. I need to give you a name because I can't pronounce whatever that was. If you're from Vega, how about Vera?"

"That will work," the robotic translation said. "I am Vera."

I always tried to look people in the eyes when I spoke to them, but I was used to the mouth being underneath. Watching her mouth move above her eyes was disconcerting and made me feel like I was hanging upside down. I was glad that we were at least on a first name basis now, though.

"May I touch your skin?" Vera asked.

Super creepy question, but I had to admit I was curious, too. "Sure."

Vera reached out and touched my arm. And then I reached out and touched hers. She looked like she would feel rubbery and weird, but she felt okay. Different, but okay. It reminded me of the time we were at the zoo and they let us all line up to touch a snake. I'd expected it to be slimy and gross, but it wasn't. Things aren't always what you'd expect.

A bird chirped loudly outside my window and Vera jumped a foot into the air like a startled cat.

"What was that?" she asked, neck-eyes bulging.

"That's a bird. No reason to be afraid."

"You have other species on this planet?"

"Yes, millions."

Vera pointed at the window. "Is that species predatory?"

"Only to worms."

"Please explain," Vera said, still nervous.

I chuckled. "Not to us. Don't worry about it." But speaking of predatory things. "What was up with that other alien last night?"

Vera's shoulders sagged. "Our home has multiple species, just like you and your birds."

"How does it differ from you?"

"My species is known for its intelligence and curiosity."

"And its?"

"They are known for their propensity toward violence."

Oh, wonderful. We had the serial killer of aliens hiding somewhere in town. Fantastic.

Vera sadly shook her giant blockhead. "We would never have brought him to your planet on purpose. I don't know how any of this happened."

I waved my hand. "I know. It's not your fault." Then I stopped. "Wait, we?"

"Yes, the group I came with."

There was a group?! I'd thought I only had to deal with two! They had to go back. Immediately. Enough with the Intergalactic United Nations meeting. Time to get down to business.

"Okay, where's your spaceship?" I asked.

Vera looked at me in confusion.

"Your UFO? Your . . . " My hands flew through the air, and I made weird airplane noises.

"*Ahh*," Vera said, finally understanding. "We have no . . . space ship."

"Then how did you travel here?"

"You."

"What do you mean, me?" I'd summoned her UFO; we'd already established that. But I didn't have it hidden in the garage or anything.

"You brought us via your communications device." She pointed again at the phone in my hand.

"Are you saying that I . . . teleported you?"

"Yes, that translates accordingly."

"But if you have no spaceship, how are you going to get back to your planet?"

"That's why I came to you. We need to go home. Since you brought me here, you can send me back."

"Well, then we have a problem," I said. "Because I have no idea how to do that."

Footsteps clambered up the stairs, and my mom's voice carried down the hall. "Bexley? I'm coming in."

8

"et in the closet!" I whisper-yelled at Vera.

Thankfully *closet* translated correctly.

Vera had just sunk into my pile of shoes and closed the door when Mom poked her head into the room.

"You're up," she said, gazing with confusion at the sight of me standing in the middle of my room in my pajamas.

I realized that my blanket and sheets were still piled on the floor from my abrupt launch out of bed. "I'm, um, making the bed."

"Well, are you up for some company? Because Charlie's here to see you."

I gulped. Charlie, who had a morning football game. A game I'd promised to go to.

"Yeah, sure, send him in."

"Would you like some chicken noodle soup for lunch?"

Not really. I only ate that when I was sick. But I had to play the part. "That sounds great. Thanks, Mom."

She left smiling, and Charlie stomped into the room, not smiling.

He was still wearing his Wolcott football jersey, and his blond hair was sticking straight up from all the sweat. His face was dirty and red and scrunched up in anger.

"Listen," he said between gritted teeth. "I know you're not a big fan of me joining the team. But today's game was important to me. I needed a friendly face in the stands. I thought my supposed best friend would be there!"

"But—"

He interrupted, "Did you hear that Robbie got hurt? I ended up playing! In my first game! I was so nervous. And you weren't there."

I put one hand on my hip. "I have a pretty good excuse."

He huffed. "I don't want to hear it. Unless you were in the hospital, nothing else excuses you."

I'd have to just show him. That would be easier than trying to explain. I calmly walked to my closet and opened the door. Vera peered out from between the hangers.

Charlie's red face turned ghastly white. "Is that an alien in your closet?"

"Yes, it is," I said. "But don't worry, she's friendly."

"Okay, you're excused." He slowly sat down on the end of my bed, his face frozen in shock.

"Vera, this is Charlie. You can trust him." I motioned with my hand for her to come out of the closet. She did, slowly, her neck eyes focused on him.

"You are sure he is a friend?" she asked.

Charlie's mouth dropped open as he looked from Vera to my phone and back again.

"Oh, yeah," I said. "The *Alien Invasion* game also

works as an alien translator. You get used to the robot voice after a while."

I put a gentle hand on Vera's shoulder. "And, yes, Charlie is my *best* friend."

Then I turned to Charlie. "This is Vera. Actually, her name is more like a bunch of dolphin sounds, but I named her Vera because she came from a planet near the star Vega."

Charlie looked up at me. "The star we were look-ing at last night?"

"Yeah. About that . . . " I proceeded to tell him how my *Alien Invasion* game had somehow teleported Vera and others to our planet. To our town, specifi-cally, because they were drawn to my mobile device.

As I spoke, Vera explored my room, staring at my posters and looking through my books.

When I finished filling Charlie in, he asked, "Can you just . . ." he mimed tapping the LASER button on the phone.

"I tried that last night when the scary alien with the bad hair tried to kill me. I was hoping it would get zapped away like the monsters, but the game did nothing to it."

Charlie nodded, taking it all in. "So we have Vera,

who is good, and another alien who is bad. What's that one's name?"

I looked at Vera, who'd taken a sock out of my dresser drawer and decided to try it on her hand.

"His name does not translate," she said, ripping the sock off and stuffing it back in the drawer.

"Bob," Charlie said.

I chuckled. "Why Bob?"

"It makes him sound less scary."

That made sense. "Okay. So who are all the others you're with?" I asked Vera.

"They are my class," Vera stated simply.

"Wait, you're a teacher?" I asked.

She opened another drawer and peered inside. "Yes, and I had students with me."

"So the other aliens here in town are kids?" Charlie asked.

"Yes, that is correct. And this particular class is . . . mischievous. They would not listen to me when we arrived on Earth. They all ran off to make trouble."

Uh-oh. That didn't sound good. I still didn't understand why, out of all the aliens on her planet, my cell phone teleported her class. "Were you in school when it happened?"

She pulled my training bra out of the drawer and held it up in the air. "What is this?"

I dashed over and grabbed the bra, stuffing it back in the drawer. Charlie was trying so hard not to laugh, I thought he'd explode.

"Can we just focus here, Vera?" I said, closing all my dresser drawers. "Where were you when you got teleported?"

She clasped her four-fingered hands in front of her in a move that looked very teacher-like. "We were on a field trip to a local observatory."

Charlie and I shared a look. That sounded familiar.

Vera continued, "We were playing with some equipment when we were involuntarily brought to this planet by you."

Again with the blame. It was an accident! But this was a bigger mess than I'd thought. A group of mischievous alien kids were loose in town, unsupervised, and running around on the greatest field trip of all time.

"How many kids were with you?" Charlie asked.

"Six," she said. "And we call ourselves . . . " A bunch of dolphin sounds came from her mouth hole. Apparently the word did not translate.

Hmm, I thought. *We'd need another name for these kids from Vega.* "We will call the rest of the kids Vegans." But as soon as I said it, I realized my mistake. "Oh, wait. That has a meaning in our language."

"That is okay," Vera said. "It translates correctly. We also don't eat other live beings or their by-products."

"Um, okay. We'll go with that, then."

Charlie fidgeted as he sat. "Was the bad alien—er, Bob—part of your class?"

Vera's pale blue skin darkened just a tad. "No. But I did see him the night of the field trip. He was skulking around the observatory, looking suspicious."

"That was why he got zapped, too," I said. "He was close by."

Charlie scratched at his chin, deep in thought. "Do you have any idea why he'd be hanging around there?"

Vera bowed her head, which I think was her way of nodding. "His species is known for hating science and all that it stands for."

Charlie gasped, as if she'd said someone didn't like candy.

Vera continued, "His species has been known to destroy instruments of science."

"So he might have been there to ruin the observatory?" I asked.

"That is my thought, yes," Vera said.

"He'd better stay away from *our* observatory," said Charlie, with fire in his eyes.

I thought about the beautiful building and how nice the astronomer, Dr. Maria, had been. I straightened my shoulders. "We have to warn them."

After a quick brainstorming session, we decided to tell my parents that Charlie had "forgotten" a notebook in the observatory on the field trip. And it couldn't wait because we needed it to study together for a test this weekend. We only needed a ride there and back. We'd be super quick. Thankfully, Dad bought our story and agreed to be our chauffeur.

So I jumped in the shower and quickly got dressed.

Then I snuck back into my room and eased open the closet door. Vera was sitting crossed legged on the floor with one of my textbooks open on her lap.

I tapped on the *Alien Invasion* app so we'd be able to talk.

"This one is the same," Vera said, pointing at the book excitedly. "I need no translation."

I looked down and smiled. Math. The universal language.

"You can read it all you want while I'm gone. I brought you a glass of water." I pointed to the glass sitting on my desk. "Is there any food you would like?" I mean, I was craving tacos, but I didn't know if that would be up an alien's alley.

"I only require water and citrus-based vitamin C."

I paused. "Like oranges?"

She paused a moment. "Yes, that translates into something I would enjoy eating."

"Okay, I think we have some downstairs. I'll be back."

I darted down the stairs and into the kitchen. Mom always kept a big bowl of fresh fruit on the counter. I usually ignored it but was glad to find it full now. I grabbed an orange from the top.

"You made a quick recovery," Mom said.

I spun around. "I think I was just tired and needed some extra sleep. I'm growing and all that."

Mom balanced an empty laundry basket on her hip. "Okay, well, I'm glad you're up and about. While Dad drives you to the observatory, I'm going to do some laundry."

Panic gripped me. "Not mine!"

Mom looked at me like I'd grown an extra head. "Why not?"

"My room is too messy right now," I said, trying my best to seem nonchalant. *Nope, not hiding an alien in there.* "I don't have all my dirty clothes in the hamper yet. I'll organize this afternoon."

"Oh, well, okay," Mom said, but she still looked at me weirdly.

Dad sauntered into the kitchen and grabbed his keys from the counter. "Ready to go?"

"Yeah, I just have to"— *bring this orange to the alien in my room* —"get my phone. I left it upstairs."

I quickly gave Vera the orange and closed my door, wishing it had a lock. I could only hope that Mom stayed out of there and Vera stayed hidden.

Charlie was waiting for us in the driveway. "Thanks for the ride, Mr. Grayson!"

"No problem," my dad said, starting the engine. "How was your game this morning?"

"We were winning," Charlie began. "And then we weren't."

The way he stared down at his shoes made me think that things took a turn for the worse when Robbie had to leave the game and Charlie was put in. I really wished I'd been there for him. But, you know, aliens in town and all that.

Dad and Charlie talked about football for most of the ride. It was so strange for Charlie to be this sports dude now. At least my dad seemed to be enjoying it. I did my best to smile and try to act like I wasn't completely bored by the conversation. Luckily, it wasn't too long before we were pulling into the parking lot of the observatory.

"We'll be quick!" I called, practically jumping out of my dad's car.

Charlie followed, catching up with me as I reached the main door and found it locked. "What are we going to do?"

I frowned. "There are other cars here. It must be closed to the public today but open for work. Let's knock."

I rapped my knuckles on the door, gently at first. When I got no answer, I ramped it up, banging on the glass with my fist.

Finally, a shadow came toward us. I tensed, worried for a split second that it could be Bob, his hands full of alien dynamite, ready to destroy the place. But I let out a breath when I saw that it was Dr. Maria, the exact person we'd wanted to see.

But she didn't seem as happy to see us.

She turned the lock on the door and opened it, just enough for her face to peek out. "What are you doing here?"

"Um," Charlie began. "We need to come inside and talk to you."

Dr. Maria shook her head. "I'm afraid I can't do that."

"Why not?" I asked.

Dr. Maria looked surprised. "You didn't hear? Wolcott Middle School is banned from the observatory. You're not allowed through this door ever again."

"Why?" I asked again. "I know some kids pushed each other there at the end, but—"

Dr. Maria cut in. "There was pushing and shoving. Our multi-million dollar telescope got banged around. Someone stomped on the planetary weight scale and broke it." Her face turned down in disgust. "And there were strange-looking boogers smeared on our meteorite."

Wow, I had no idea my class had been that bad. But still, it wasn't Charlie and me. "But we weren't the kids who misbehaved!" I argued.

She narrowed her eyes at me. "You bumped into the telescope and nearly wrecked my device with your phone."

Okay, point taken. Though that wasn't my fault. I was pushed.

"Listen," Charlie tried. "This is important. We need to talk to you about your machine and *real* aliens here on Earth. There's a bad—"

Dr. Maria put up a hand and shook her head. "I'm really sorry, kids. I truly am. I'm glad you're so interested, but I simply can't speak with you. It's a liability issue. I could lose my job."

I looked at Charlie and shook my head. We had to back off. I'd already accidentally summoned aliens to town. I didn't need to get Dr. Maria fired, too. I started to walk away, shoulders sagging.

"One quick question," Charlie said, pleading. "Please?"

Dr. Maria heaved a sigh and glanced over her shoulder. "Okay, but hurry."

"Have you seen anyone or any*thing* hanging around since last night? Acting suspicious?"

She smirked, like we were two crazy kids with overactive imaginations. "No. Only you two. Now go home."

With mixed feelings, I walked back to the car. I was frustrated that Dr. Maria wouldn't help us or even talk to us, really. But the good news was that Bob hadn't been spotted. And since I'd seen him in my backyard last night, he was probably nowhere near the observatory. He was closer to home.

My stomach turned as I realized that probably wasn't good news after all.

10

We got back to the car, notebook-less, and told my dad that it wasn't there. Then Charlie "remembered" leaving it in a drawer at home. I hated lying to my dad, who was being really cool about everything. But there are levels of cool, and allowing me to keep an alien in my closet was probably one level above what my dad would put up with.

Dad parked the car and went into the house while Charlie and I stayed outside to game-plan.

"So what now?" Charlie asked.

"I have no idea," I said, frustration leaking into my voice. "All I know is that I brought those aliens here, so it's my responsibility to see them home."

"See them . . . " Charlie repeated slowly. "I wonder if everyone can see them? Or just people who play *Alien Invasion?*"

"Hmm. I don't know." It was a good question. When *Monsters Unleashed* had accidentally unleashed monsters into town, only people who'd played the game could see them. But things seemed different this time. These weren't video-game aliens. They were real aliens who'd been living real lives before they were teleported here.

Charlie's older brother, Jason, came out of their house and started pacing the front yard. Jason was only two years older, but he was double our size. He had a buzz cut and shoulders as wide as a doorway, which together made him look pretty intimidating. But I'd watched him nearly pee himself as a monster held him six feet in the air, so that took some of the fear away.

Now, he walked toward us, running his fingers along the back of his head like he was searching for buried treasure.

"Um, what are you doing?" Charlie asked.

"Looking for a bump on my head," Jason answered.

"Did you hit your head?" I asked.

"Not that I can remember, but I think I have a concussion. Maybe there was a play in practice that was rougher than I remember."

Charlie frowned. "If you don't remember getting hurt, why do you think you have a concussion?"

Jason stopped rubbing his head and stared at us. "You have to promise not to tell Mom. She'll just freak out and make me get another MRI, and I've had, like, twelve of those this year. It's getting boring."

Charlie nodded. "I promise."

Jason took a deep breath. "I thought I saw an alien in our backyard."

My heart skipped a beat in my chest. Had Vera run away? Or had my mom found her? Oh, gosh, what happened?

"An alien?" Charlie repeated, keeping his voice level.

"Yeah. It was blue and had three legs and a really bad haircut."

All the breath I'd been holding came out in a *whoosh*. Vera was still safely inside. Jason had seen Bob. Which was both good and bad.

Charlie's finger shot into the air. "I think I have it figured out!"

"You do?" Jason said.

"You do?" I said, even louder. I didn't want him to tell Jason about our little alien problem quite yet. I didn't want anyone to know until we had the situation under control.

"Who are we playing against next week?" Charlie said. "Runswick, right?"

Jason's eyes lit up. "The Runswick Martians!" He shook his head. "Those jerks. They're dressing up and trying to scare our best players." He pointed at himself, in case the implication wasn't clear.

I had to hold back a giggle. I'd always thought that Runswick had the dumbest team name ever. Though, as the Wolcott Devils, we didn't exactly get points for creativity. But Charlie's quick thinking had saved us in the moment. It was a relief to know he and I were on the same page about telling Jason—that we were still on the same page about something.

Jason took off, grumbling about revenge.

"We'll get our revenge on the field next week!" Charlie called.

When we were alone again, I turned to Charlie. "Well, now we know two things."

"One," Charlie said. "Anyone can see the aliens."

"And two," I added. "Bob isn't interested in the observatory. Whatever he wants is around here."

Charlie nodded somberly. Then he glanced at the time on his phone. "I have to go."

"Really?" I said, surprised. "You don't want to come see Vera again?" I mean, for a science geek like Charlie, having a real life alien next door must have felt like opportunity of a lifetime.

"I would, but I have an appointment." He smiled huge. "My braces are coming off."

"Oh, I didn't know that was happening." Poor Charlie had had braces on his teeth for nearly three years, so I should've been delighted for him to finally get them off. But instead I felt strange. Like this was yet another change coming at me too quickly. And I'd noticed he'd grown a bit, too. He was finally taller than I was. Charlie was changing inside and out.

"Text me later," he said, running off.

"Hey!" I called out. "Got any science jokes for me before you go?"

He stopped and shrugged. "I don't really think those up anymore."

I sulked back into my house and upstairs to my room. Vera was safely in my closet, on the last page of my math book, orange peels littering the floor. I opened the *Alien Invasion* app and asked, "Everything good here?"

"Yes," Vera's robotic translation said. "No problems. But I would like another math textbook."

I sank onto the end of my bed. "Okay, I'll put that on the list with more oranges and a bigger brain to figure out how to help you get home."

Vera frowned and climbed out of the closet, flinging a shoe out of her way. "Bex, my friend. You seem sad. Did Bob destroy your favorite observatory?"

"No. He wasn't there. Charlie's brother actually saw him skulking around the backyard again."

Vera's face darkened. "He is planning something. He is no good."

A knock came on the door. My dad's voice called, "Can I come in?"

Vera's neck eyes bulged in fear.

"No!" I cried. "Not right now."

"Why not?" Dad asked, suspicion in his voice.

Because I have an alien in my room really wasn't a non-suspicious answer. But a thought occurred to me. Something he would understand.

"I need to 'decompress' from our trip to the observatory," I said, using his favorite word.

"Oh." He sounded kind of stunned. "Sure. Of course."

Vera nodded at me, impressed, then headed back to her spot in the closet.

I smiled huge. It worked! But I couldn't keep my parents out of my room forever. And this problem seemed to be lasting longer than I'd originally thought it would. Vera couldn't stay here too much longer. I'd have to figure out another solution.

A shoe that had apparently gotten in Vera's way launched past my head and hit the wall behind me.

And that solution had to come soon.

11

After I had dinner with my parents and snuck Vera a couple more oranges, I spent the rest of the night in my room with her, playing with the *Alien Invasion* game, trying to find any way that it could send her home. The game functions still worked normally. It was strange to show Vera, an actual alien, how the point of the game was to shoot fictional aliens, though I think she understood that it wasn't real, and I'd never hurt her.

I tossed and turned overnight as nightmare after nightmare tortured my brain. Vera in danger from people. Bob trying to kill me again. The little Vegans getting hurt. I woke up the next morning covered in sweat.

After my shower and a quick breakfast, I heard a knock on the front door. The last person I expected to see stood there, arms crossed, foot tapping, an expectant look on her face.

"Good morning, Willa," I said sarcastically. "How are you on this lovely day?"

"What did you and Charlie do now?" she snapped. "And why didn't you tell me?"

I coughed into my hand. "Wh-what are you talking about?"

She threw her arms up into the air. "You let the monsters out again! I thought we all agreed that we wouldn't play that game anymore."

Thankfully my parents were at the grocery store. I opened the door wide and let Willa in. She followed me to the kitchen.

"Monsters?" I asked, legitimately confused. "What monsters? They're not loose again."

Willa gave me a disbelieving look. "Then how do

you explain Bodhi's Diner? It was so wrecked, they couldn't open for breakfast. And I really wanted their blueberry pancakes!"

I eased onto a chair at the kitchen island. "Okay, slow down. What happened to the restaurant?"

"Someone or some*thing* broke in overnight and made a huge mess. They put chairs on top of tables. They tossed flour all over the place like fake snow. And they ate all the fruit! Every last orange for the morning juice. Every last blueberry for the pancakes. And you know how I know it wasn't a human?"

"How?"

"They left all the money untouched in the register's drawer. So, admit it." She narrowed her eyes and stared me down.

"Fine," I relented. "We have a problem. But it's not monsters. It's aliens."

Willa's eyebrows rose halfway up her forehead. "Now there's a twist I didn't see coming."

"Believe me. I was taken by surprise as well."

Willa's lips formed a small pout. "But why didn't you and Charlie tell me? I thought that after this summer . . . "

Her voice trailed off, but I knew what she meant.

After dumping me and bullying me for a year or so, she'd apologized this past summer and we were slowly becoming friends again. But that wouldn't happen overnight. I needed more time. I didn't want to get into all of that with her right now, though.

Instead, I said, "Let me text Charlie. He has to come over and hear about the diner."

This was our first clue to the Vegans' whereabouts. Five minutes later, Charlie came flying through the front door and we all went upstairs for introductions.

"Willa, this is Vera. Vera, this is Willa."

I'd gotten so used to Vera's upside down eyes and mouth that I hadn't thought to warn Willa and, of course, she didn't try to hide the shock on her face. She pointed a shaky finger. "Her eyes . . . in her neck . . . "

"Yes, anyway," I spoke over her. "Willa goes to my school."

"Is she a friend to be trusted?" Vera asked. "Like Charlie?"

"No, not a friend," I said, without even thinking. Out of the corner of my eye I saw Willa's face fall and felt a stab of guilt. "But she knows about you, and she has our first clue to the whereabouts of the other Vegans."

Willa crossed her arms. "So how many aliens are we dealing with here?"

"Eight," I answered. "There's Vera, her class of six young Vegans, and the alien we're calling Bob. The Vegans aren't evil. They didn't mean to wreck the restaurant. They're just mischievous."

"And what about this Bob?"

"Oh, he's evil," Charlie said. "And violent."

"Fantastic," Willa said with a groan.

"So should we head to the diner and see if one of the Vegans is still there?" I asked.

"There will be two," Vera said, matter-of-factly.

"Interesting." Charlie leaned forward with fascination. "Is that a mandate in your species?"

"No. But we use the buddy system on field trips. The children may be mischievous but they would never break that one rule."

I paced back and forth, my feet echoing on the hardwood floor. "Okay, so let's say there are two there and we catch them. We can't bring them all to my room."

"I was thinking about that," Charlie said. "We can't keep Vera in here much longer either. But . . . Grandpa Tepper is away for a week."

"Where did he go?" Charlie's grandpa was one of my favorite people in the world. I thought it was strange that he'd gone somewhere and I hadn't heard about it.

Charlie's cheeks reddened. "He went on an over-seventy singles' cruise."

Willa and I burst out laughing—bent over, grabbing our sides, uncontrollable laughing.

"What?" Charlie snapped. "It's not funny."

"Oh, yeah, it is," Willa said between gasps of laughter.

He scowled. "I don't want to think about my old grandfather on some cruise on the prowl for a new woman."

I stopped laughing and went to Charlie's side. "Your grandmother has been gone for ten years," I said softly. "He's all alone in that big house. Maybe he'll meet someone he really likes."

Charlie softened. "I mean, yeah, but . . . I just don't want to think about it."

A change in subject would be good right about now, I thought. "Anyway, that's a great idea, but the little Vegans will destroy Grandpa Tepper's house. We can't do that to him."

"Then how about his garage?" Charlie suggested. "It's pretty much empty now that he can't drive anymore and doesn't own a car. We can put a bunch of blankets and pillows in there. Some balls and stuff for them to play with."

"More math textbooks?" Vera asked hopefully.

"Yes," I said. "And dozens of oranges!"

"And I know how to get them there," Willa said, raising a finger into the air. "My parents have an old double stroller in the basement from when the twins were little. They wouldn't notice if we took that out for a spin."

The plan was all coming together. I clapped my hands. "Okay, so we head to the diner. We find two Vegans, get them in the stroller, cover them with baby blankets, and bring them to Grandpa Tepper's garage."

Vera stepped into the circle that Willa, Charlie, and I had made. "There is a problem. The children will not go with you. They will not trust you unless they see me."

The three of us looked at one another. How were we going to bring a four-foot alien downtown?

"his is a bad idea," I said.

Willa tossed her hair over one shoulder. "Relax. I saw it in a movie."

Charlie looked to the left and right as we walked out my front door. "Yeah, I saw that same movie, and the only reason it worked was because it was Halloween. Vera's not exactly going to blend in on a pleasant September morning wearing a full-length winter coat and ski mask."

Willa stopped and stared at Charlie. "You got your braces off."

"Yeah, yesterday afternoon," Charlie said.

I cringed, waiting for the insult that would inevitably follow.

"Looks good," Willa said. And that's all she said.

"Anyway . . . " I said, moving past that slice of weirdness. "I still think this is crazy."

Willa pushed the double stroller she'd gotten from her house. Charlie and I walked behind her, each holding one of Vera's hands. The disguise covered her blue skin, and the long coat even made it so that you couldn't see that she had three legs. But it was still super-suspicious looking. We just had to hope we didn't attract any attention as we walked to the diner.

I had the *Alien Invasion* app open in case Vera needed to speak with us, but we'd instructed her not to talk at all in front of strangers. Wearing a long coat and ski mask on a mild fall day was strange enough without having a robot voice.

As we passed Mrs. Sweeney's house, William Shakespaw began barking out the window as furiously as I'd ever seen him. William was a small white puffball of a dog and was normally very chill. That probably had a lot to do with him being sixteen years old, which was a bazillion in dog years. He never barked at kids walking by his house. So Vera's disguise definitely wasn't tricking him.

Vera's hand trembled in mine. "What is that?"

"That's a dog," I explained. "Um, canine is the formal name, I think."

"Is it dangerous? Or benevolent like the bird species?"

"Some dogs can bite, but not William Shakespaw. He's the nicest dog ever."

"According to your communication device's translation, the small furry species would like us to move away from his property."

My eyebrows rose. My phone just translated Dog to Vera? What *couldn't* this app do?

We scurried past quickly, and Vera's tight grip on my hand loosened. Birds and small old dogs certainly weren't scary to me, but I guess if you'd never seen one before, they could be. I'd nearly peed my pants when Vera and Bob came out of the woods on Friday!

And now I nearly peed them again. We'd almost made it to the diner without anyone coming too close, but a woman and her kid were strolling down the sidewalk toward us.

"Stay cool," I reminded everyone. *This would be fine*, I tried to convince myself. They'd walk on by. Three middle schoolers, one double stroller, and a child disguised as a cold bank robber is something you totally see every day.

As they got closer, the mother looked us over but didn't say anything. Then her kid pointed to Vera and yelled, "Look at that! He's weird!"

Leave it to four year olds to just say what they're thinking.

"We're a babysitting club!" Willa practically shrieked. "Kids love playing dress up! You know how they are!"

The woman put a protective hand on her child's back, hustling him forward. I didn't blame her. Willa's forced chipper tone was scarier than her mean voice.

But at last we were at the diner. It was closed, as Willa had said, but luckily the owners' daughter, Vanya Patel, was one of my friends from school. I'd gone with her once to open the diner the morning after a sleepover and I remembered where they hid the emergency key.

A small landscaped area surrounded a pretty bench near the front door. One of the rocks was fake. I bent down, squinting, and found it. The color matched the others, but it was too smooth. I picked it up and opened the secret hatch on the back.

I held the key up in victory. "Shall we?"

"We should hurry," Willa said. "I talked to Vanya before I went to your house. After they finished cleaning up, they were heading to the store to restock the food they'd lost, then they were coming right back."

I unlocked the door, and we pushed inside. The place looked okay but smelled like cleaning products, and patches of flour were caked into the corners.

"Okay, alien friends," Charlie said, trying to use an authoritative voice. "Come out so we can help you."

I was suddenly worried that the Vegans weren't here at all. I mean, if Vanya's parents had spent the morning cleaning the diner, wouldn't the little aliens have run off? Unless they were hiding somewhere . . .

My eyes went to the cabinets beneath the counters. I marched over and knocked on the first one. A startled clicking sound echoed from a space farther down. I moved toward it and ripped open the cabinet door.

Two little aliens burst out, squealing and running

in circles around the diner. Vera was full-grown at five feet so I'd been expecting the Vegans to be small. But they were the size of toddlers!

One picked up a glass from the counter and smashed it on the ground.

Apparently they had the temperament of toddlers, too.

Vera reached her hand out to grab the closest alien's arm, but it jerked it and climbed on top of a table. It made a horrible noise like when you scrape a fork against a plate, except ten times louder.

The second alien ran up and kicked me in the shin.

"Ouch!" I yelled, doubling over and clutching my leg.

It started running for the door. *Ugh*, I thought, *now we'd have to chase it through downtown*. Not very inconspicuous!

But then Charlie jumped at the kid alien, wrapping his arms around it and tackling it to the floor.

"Impressive," Willa said, almost under her breath.

"I guess all those hours at football practice aren't for nothing," Charlie said.

I held my phone up so the Vegans could clearly

understand me. "Hey! You need to listen to your teacher!"

The alien with Charlie stopped squirming and the one dancing on the table froze in mid-move, both shocked that they were able to understand me.

"Vera," I began. "Um, your teacher, is just trying to keep you safe. Now, stop this nonsense and come with us before you get hurt."

Wow, that little speech made me feel all adult-ish. And it worked. Vera held out her hands and the little aliens each took one. I put my phone away and Vera dolphin-sounded some harsh words to the misbehaving kids as we strapped them into the stroller.

I brushed my hands off on my jeans. "Two Vegans down, four to go."

Plus, you know, Bob the alien psychopath.

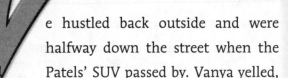

13

We hustled back outside and were halfway down the street when the Patels' SUV passed by. Vanya yelled, "Hi, Bex" out the window, and I waved back like everything was normal and I hadn't just captured two aliens from her family's restaurant. We turned down the next street, heading toward Grandpa Tepper's neighborhood, when we ran—almost literally—into Charlie's brother.

"Hey," Jason said, looking at us suspiciously.

"Heading to the game?" Charlie asked, doing a poor job of hiding the nervousness in his voice.

"Yeah." Jason narrowed his eyes. "But what are *you* doing?"

This wasn't good. We'd asked Jason not to get involved in our monster drama this past summer, and he didn't listen and nearly got himself killed. I really didn't want him involving himself with our little alien problem.

"We're babysitting!" I yelled, with a little too much enthusiasm.

Jason scoffed. "Since when? And whose kids?"

As if in response, the two Vegans started chatting away to each other in their alien language. They were about as quiet as a school bus in reverse.

Jason raised one eyebrow. "That doesn't sound like babies." Then he reached forward and snatched the blanket off the double stroller, revealing two small upside down alien faces. One of them burped right at Jason's open mouth.

I froze.

Charlie's jaw dropped open.

Willa let out a nervous giggle.

Jason straightened, his face pale. "I don't even

want to know. Not this time. Nope. I'm out." And then he continued down the road, whistling like nothing had happened.

"Well that's one less potential problem," I said, letting out a breath.

Charlie eyes focused on something over my shoulder. "But there might be another one."

I turned around, but didn't see anyone else walking down the street. "What?"

"That white van was parked outside the diner. And now it's parked here." Charlie spoke from the side of his mouth, like he didn't want anyone to read his lips. "I noticed it slow to a stop as we talked to Jason. Like it was following us."

I looked back again. It seemed like a normal van. The windows were tinted just enough that I couldn't see if anyone was in it. A plumbing company logo was on the side.

"It's a plumber," Willa said. "He goes from job to job, so of course the van is going to move. Stop looking for problems where there aren't any."

A drop of water fell onto my forehead. Oh, great. Was it going to rain? I looked up at the ominous gray sky, and another drop fell right onto my eyeball.

"Vera!" Charlie cried. "You're not allergic to water are you?"

"This is what I'm talking about," Willa said scornfully. "Looking for stupid problems. Who would be allergic to water?"

"Aliens. I saw an invasion movie once where water killed them," Charlie explained.

Willa snorted. "How dumb do aliens have to be to land on a planet that's seventy percent water if they're allergic to water?"

Charlie rolled his eyes. "Yeah, it was a total plot hole, but still—"

"You guys," I interrupted. "She drinks water. She's fine."

"Yes, I enjoy the liquid water," Vera's robot voice said.

"Okay, water's fine," Charlie continued. "But we still need to be careful when she's introduced to something new. It could be okay for humans but harmful to her. Like dogs and chocolate!"

Willa groaned. "I'm just saying you don't need to overreact to every little—"

"Can we stop bickering and move on before we get soaked?" I pushed everyone forward.

We arrived at Grandpa Tepper's garage without further incident. Charlie typed in the code to open the garage door and told it to Willa and me in case we ever needed it. The garage was pretty much empty. One corner had some house stuff—a shovel and salt for the driveway. But the rest was wide open.

Charlie grabbed some blankets and pillows from inside the house. I parked the stroller and let the alien kids out. And Willa unpacked a bag of toys she'd taken from her basement. Her twin brothers were eight now and had outgrown them.

"Math textbooks?" Vera reminded me.

"Yes, I'll get you more of those," I assured her.

"And oranges!" the Vegans yelled, jumping up and down.

"They really enjoyed the oranges from the diner," Vera explained. "They told me they ate every one. But they will need more by tomorrow."

"I'll stop by the store, too," I promised.

Charlie piled up the blankets in the corner. "You'll be safe here. But we have to go for now. We'll be back."

The three of us headed back down the driveway. I'd thought all the drama was over when we'd successfully booted all the monsters from our town. But here we were, collecting aliens. At least I had a team. I wasn't alone.

Willa pulled an elastic out of her pocket and started to pull her hair up into a bun. "I'd love to spend the afternoon with you walking disasters, but I have dance class. Later." Then she marched off in the opposite direction.

"I have to go, too," Charlie said, looking guilty. "The team is heading out to watch the varsity game together. It's the whole team, you know? Plus, my brother's playing in the game."

A lump formed in the back of my throat. "Of course."

"You don't mind doing the errands by yourself?"

I paused. Yeah, I minded. I was going to spend the rest of the day acting like an alien delivery service getting textbooks and oranges. Oh, and if I ran into any little Vegans on my way I had to somehow capture them all alone. Because watching a stupid game with his friends was more important than helping me.

But I didn't say any of that. I swallowed hard and forced out the words, "It's no problem."

Then I walked off before he could see the tears

that had formed in the corners of my eyes. Maybe I should have accepted Marcus's offer to join the Gamer Squad, after all.

"Where's your other half?"

I had just entered the library when I heard the voice of Mrs. Dorsey, my favorite librarian. She was a gamer and had been hardcore helpful with our monster problem. But right now I was trying hard not to show any emotion as I turned around to face her.

"Hey," she said, moving closer. "What's wrong? Is Charlie okay?"

I guess I shouldn't abandon my plans of becoming a programmer for a life of poker.

"Charlie's fine," I said. "Just busy. And I'm a little overwhelmed with . . . stuff."

"Anything I can help with?"

"Math textbooks."

She did a double take. "What now?"

"I need a lot of math textbooks. It doesn't matter if they're old or not."

Concern fell over her features. "I know a tutor if you need—"

"No," I said, interrupting her. "It's nothing like that. It's . . . " I lowered my voice and leaned in closer. "Just tell me if you notice anything odd. Like this-past-summer odd, if you get what I'm saying."

Her eyes widened and she nodded her head slowly. "I will, Bex. Come to me if you need anything. In the meantime, let's get those textbooks."

I headed to the grocery store next. The bag of books was starting to hurt my right shoulder, and soon I had a giant bag of oranges on the left. I really could have used some help.

The pile of oranges spilled from my hands onto the checkout belt. The cashier looked up at me from behind her wire-rimmed glasses.

"Flu season's coming," I said. "We have to get ahead of the game. Build up our immune system with some vitamin C."

She gave me a look like *sure, crazy person* and rang the oranges up. Several minutes later, I realized that I should've just said I was making my own juice. But that's what my brain did. It panicked, said weird stuff, and then thought up normal stuff when the conversation was long over. I was used to it by now.

I dropped the goodies off at Grandpa Tepper's

garage and made a bunch of aliens happy. Then I headed home. By the time I reached my street, it had started to rain again. That morning shower had been brief, but by the look of the darkening sky this was going to be a long one. I was lucky I'd finished all my errands.

My shoulders aching, I dragged myself up the driveway toward my front door. But before I reached the steps, I noticed something odd. There were foot-prints in the mud around my front bushes. I followed them and they went all the way around the house to the backdoor. Then they changed direction and went toward the backyard. Stranger still, the prints were not in pairs of two.

Something three-legged had been skulking around my house. Bob.

14

Monday morning, I rushed around the school halls looking for someone in particular. Charlie and Willa had such busy schedules, I'd decided last night that I would have to find someone else to help me catch the rest of the Vegans. And I found him leaning against the wall outside the computer lab.

"Marcus?"

He stood up straight, looking surprised to see me. "Oh, hey, Bex."

I could tell Marcus about the aliens. He'd believe me. And he might even have some solid ideas how to help. But first, I had to make sure he wasn't still upset. I hated to think that Marcus was mad at me for not joining the group. Not because I had a huge, raging crush on him (though I did), but because I didn't like *anyone* to be mad at me.

"I hope you're not still upset about—"

He shook his head quickly before I could finish the sentence. "You have the right to join or not join whatever club you want."

"Okay." I smiled sheepishly. "Is everyone else mad?"

"Everyone else?" he repeated.

"The rest of the Gamer Squad," I whispered. Then, out of curiosity, I asked, "Who else is in the group, anyway?"

"I can't tell you that," he said quickly, guarding their identities like it was the World's Biggest Secret.

"Oh, okay," I said with a shrug, trying my best to make it look like I didn't care. But I did. Even more so because of how secretive he'd been. I really wanted to know who else was in the group. Maybe they could help.

But before I could even start to tell him about the

alien issue, he blurted out, "Look, I really need to get to class," and took off down the hall.

The bell rang soon after, and then I had to try to push my problems to the back of my mind and pull schoolwork to the front. Easier said than done. Turns out it's hard to concentrate when you're hiding a bunch of aliens in your best friend's grandfather's garage.

In science class, Mr. Durr got sidetracked talking about the possibility of wormholes in space. That guy *loved* science, and he tried his best to get students enthusiastic about it, too. Aside from his penchant for annoying pop quizzes and his dorky "Funny Tie Fridays," he was my favorite teacher. And that was how, after the last school bell rang, I ended up outside his classroom.

One of Willa's friends was already in there, getting extra help for the test later in the week. I waited patiently for my turn. She came out, gave my outfit the once over, and wrinkled her nose. Then Mr. Durr called out, "Next!"

I entered the classroom and closed the door behind me.

"Bexley?" Mr. Durr said with surprise. "How can I help you?"

I took a seat opposite his desk and fiddled with a pencil someone had left there. "Um, it's not about science really. Or not anything we're going over right now."

He looked at me over the top of his eyeglasses. "Okay . . . "

"I'm writing this short story," I began. "And it's about aliens. But I want to make it as realistic as possible."

He rubbed his hands together. "I'd love to help. What question do you have?"

I opened my mouth to speak, but then a strange bumping sound came from the ceiling over my head. I looked up and saw nothing—just ceiling tiles.

"It's the air ducts," Mr. Durr said. "They really need to get the HVAC system tuned up before we need to turn on the heat." He shook his head in judgment. "Anyway, continue."

I cleared my throat. "In my story, some aliens land on Earth. Not to, like, invade us or anything. They didn't even mean to come here. But now they're kind of stuck. My main character is a human who is trying to help them. What should she do?"

He snorted. "She should run for the hills!"

"What?" I blurted. "Why?"

"Aliens could be carrying viruses or bacteria that our immune systems are not prepared to handle, and they could infect—"

I interrupted. "Okay, but let's say it's been a couple days and everything seems cool. Then, what would you do to help the aliens get back home?"

"It would be best to turn any alien over to the appropriate government agency."

"Would they find a way to get her home? Or, um, it, home?"

He shook his head. "Definitely not."

Dread formed in the center of my belly. "What would they do?"

"Perform experiments. Try to find out as much as they could about the alien's biology and psychology. And then, eventually, an autopsy. It would be a great learning opportunity."

I pictured Vera tied down to some stretcher. Surgical-masked men leaning over her with instruments of torture. Needles. Pain. The little Vegans held in cages, crying for their beloved teacher.

"Did you hear me?" Mr. Durr said, breaking into my horrifying vision.

"Sorry, what?"

"I asked if you needed to know anything else."

"Oh, no. Thank you. That's everything I need to know."

I had to keep Vera and the others a secret. Accident or not, I brought them here. I was responsible. I would find a way to safely get them back home. I couldn't risk some agency grabbing them. Well, they could have Bob. But Bob would give up the others in a second. The Vegans were mischievous little jerks, but I didn't want them cut up and experimented on. Just the thought of it made my breath go ragged. I had to save them all.

I wandered back into the hall, lost in my own thoughts, when a hand clamped down on my arm.

"Bex," Marcus said, his hazel eyes flaring with intensity. "There's something you need to see."

15

arcus led me down the hallway, moving so fast I had to almost jog to keep up with his long strides.

"Where are we going?" I asked between ragged breaths.

"The boys' locker room."

"What? Why?"

"You'll see."

We careened around the corner and found various members of the middle school football team hanging in the hall. They should have been in the locker room getting dressed for practice. Actually, by now they should have been done in the locker room. They should have been out on the field.

"What's going on?" I asked, just as the door to the locker room opened and one more student came out, his face twisted in anger. Before the door closed shut, I was able to see inside the room. It was a disaster—benches flipped over, clothing strewn about, toilet paper from the bathroom draped around like ugly birthday streamers.

"The locker room got wrecked," Marcus said. "I asked around. It was fine during gym class in fifth period, but when the football team came after the last bell, it looked like that."

"So it happened sometime in the last two periods of the school day," I said, thinking out loud.

Robbie had been pacing back and forth but now stopped beside me. "My locker door was ripped right off its hinges."

"Wow," I said. "Just yours?"

"Yeah. I don't know why whoever did it targeted me. Maybe because I'm the QB. But how would they even know which locker was mine?"

"Was anything stolen?" I asked.

Robbie shook his head. "Nothing important, just the bag of orange slices my mom packs for me every day."

I swallowed hard. "Did you find anything, um, I mean anyone in there?"

"No," Robbie said. "And they couldn't have been hiding because we checked every locker, every stall, every corner. They came in, wrecked the place, and got out."

Robbie wandered off to talk with other team members. I found Charlie's eyes in the crowd. He looked concerned, but I could tell he had an idea about what was going on. With the information about the orange slices, I was pretty sure myself.

"We're going to make them pay," Robbie yelled suddenly.

The rest of the team cried, "Yeah!"

"They're going to be sorry that they messed with us!" Robbie held his arm up. "Wolcott on three. One, two, three."

"Wolcott!" The team screamed, arms raised in the air.

"They think the Runswick Martians did it for a school rivalry prank," Marcus explained, "to kind of freak them out before the big game."

I bet I knew who suggested that theory. I glanced at Charlie, who shrugged in response.

"But I don't think it's true," Marcus said.

My head whipped back toward him. "Why?"

"Things don't add up. The school day in Runswick ends at the same time as ours. They wouldn't have had enough time to get here and wreck the locker room before our bell rang and the team went inside. Plus, pulling a locker door off its hinge?" He leaned closer and lowered his voice. "That smells like monster trouble to me."

The football coach came out of the locker room and led the team outside. Charlie gave me one last look over his shoulder. I knew he wished he could help. But he couldn't walk out of practice.

Marcus, however, was close enough to the truth. Time to bring him into the circle.

I let out a deep breath. "Come with me."

The halls were eerily empty, as most of the other students had left. The school buses had come and gone. A couple teachers remained in their classrooms, grading papers. The Debate Club argued in the library about how much time to give a response.

"Where are we going?" Marcus asked.

"The cafeteria," I said. "I'll explain when we get there."

The Vegans were clearly responsible for the locker room fiasco and while they weren't in there anymore, they couldn't have gone far. Robbie's locker made a couple things clear—the little aliens were surprisingly strong, and they were hunting for vitamin C. If they could follow their alien senses to the slices in Robbie's locker, it made sense that they'd head for the cafeteria next. It would be cleared out now, all the employees gone home.

Mrs. Kemmerer, a social studies teacher, was leaving her classroom, arms piled high with overstuffed folders. She had a confused look on her face, and when she saw Marcus and me, she asked, "Did you see that?"

I stopped in mid-stride. "See what?"

"A small child just went tearing down the hall in a very realistic alien costume." She shook her head. "I'm sure the parents paid a lot of money for a costume that high end. That child shouldn't be playing around in it now, with Halloween still a month away."

Marcus pointed toward the cafeteria. "Did the, uh, child go that way?"

"Yes." She frowned. "But I haven't seen a parent. That child is definitely too young to be a student here."

"We'll keep an eye out," I said, tugging Marcus away by his sleeve. We had to get to the Vegans before they attracted any more attention.

I pushed the heavy swinging door to the cafeteria. I'd never been in there after school. I was used to the bright fluorescent bulbs and the chaotic sounds of a hundred conversations at once. I squinted through the dim light as my sneakers echoed in the silence.

"Bex, what is going on?" Marcus asked in hushed tone.

I led us around the freezer of ice cream treats and behind the counters where we lined up for hot lunch. "Where do you think they keep the fruit?"

Marcus scratched his head. "Huh?"

"Fresh fruit, like oranges and stuff."

He pointed to the far corner of the room. "Maybe in that giant steel fridge that should be closed but isn't?"

I spun around. Yep, that fridge looked like somewhere they'd store fruit. And the door was left open. So either the Vegans stole and ran. Or . . . they were still inside.

"Stay behind me," I said.

I advanced slowly, trying to keep my sneakers from squeaking on the waxed floor. If the aliens were in that fridge, I had no idea what to do with them. I didn't have Willa's stroller. I didn't have Vera with me to convince them to behave. All I had was my phone to translate. I glanced down and made sure the app was open. The fridge was closer now. So close, I could almost see around the open door.

"What are we doing?" Marcus asked, too loudly. "Will you *please* tell me what's going on?"

Two Vegans jumped out of the giant fridge, and piles of fruit and food came with them, toppling to the floor. They must have been deep in there, gorging themselves. They both smelled like citrus and one of them even had mushy remnants of an orange all over his little mouth.

I reached out to grab the closest alien before it could run past me. I got a good hold on its arm, and strangely enough it didn't struggle. Its face looked weird, though, like something else was about to happen. And then its mouth opened widely in the center of its head, and it projectile-vomited mushy, half-digested oranges all over my shirt.

"Yuck!" I cried, automatically releasing its arm. It scurried away with the other alien, who'd backed up into a corner of the room.

I spoke as clearly as I could into my phone. "We mean you no harm. Your teacher sent us to save you."

Marcus jumped in front of me. "I've got this!" he yelled, pulling out his phone and opening the *Alien Invasion* game.

"That won't work," I said.

He stabbed at the screen with his finger. "Nothing's happening to them. It's not working!"

"Am I talking to myself here?" I rolled my eyes. "It's different this time. They're not the same as the monsters."

While Marcus and I were distracted for a couple seconds, the Vegans climbed up on top of a storage unit.

"What are you doing up there?" I called. "Get down! We need to bring you to safety."

They blinked their neck eyes at me, understanding but not trusting. The one who'd puked on me simply said, "No." Then it kicked out the vent cover and one after the other, they jumped up into the air ducts.

Now I knew what that noise had been in Mr.

Durr's classroom. The HVAC system had a bigger problem than he thought.

This was *not* good. I dragged my fingers through my hair. "We can't fit into the air duct. And we're going to attract attention if we stay here any longer. We'll have to come back later with a plan." I groaned. "They'll never come to me without Vera. But I can't bring Vera into school. Oh, what should I do?"

"I actually think you *are* talking to yourself," Marcus said.

My shoulders sagged. "Sorry. I'm a little overwhelmed at the moment." I risked a glance at him. Strangely, he was looking at me the way boys normally looked at Willa. I couldn't understand why. Sweat was rolling down my forehead and my shirt was covered in alien barf. Not ideal for when you're hanging with your crush.

He pointed up at the ceiling. "Are there really aliens hiding in our school air ducts right now? Is that what I just saw?"

"Yes. I have a lot to tell you. But it's actually easier to show you. Do you have any plans this afternoon?"

He smiled widely. "I do now."

As we walked to Grandpa Tepper's garage, I brought Marcus up to speed with Wolcott's real life alien invasion. From the night at the observatory to evil Bob, I told him every detail.

"How is this happening again?" he asked, eyes wide.

I shook my head. "I don't know. I must be some sort of jinx or bad luck charm."

He gave me a look. "I don't believe that."

"Well, in any case, I have to find them all—

including the psychopath—and figure out a way to send them back home."

We stopped at the bottom of Grandpa Tepper's driveway. Marcus put his hand on my arm, and it made me feel all weird and lightheaded.

"Don't worry," he said. "I'll help you."

I was scared that if I opened my mouth at that moment, any possible combination of words could tumble out, like: I'VE HAD A CRUSH ON YOU FOR-EVER! Or YOUR HAZEL EYES ARE SO DREAMY I COULD STARE AT THEM ALL DAY. So I just pointed at the garage door and grunted. *Super cute behavior.*

I typed in the code Charlie had given me, and the door whirred to life and began to rise.

"They're nice, right?" Marcus asked nervously.

"The ones that are in there, yeah." I pointed to the bag he held in his hand. "Don't worry. They'll love you."

Before we left the cafeteria, we'd scooped up whatever fruit was left and put it in a plastic bag. I had the idea to let Marcus hand it out, to earn the trust of Vera and the little Vegans.

The door reached the top and Marcus gasped at the sight before him. Vera sat on a blanket reading a math textbook. The two little Vegans circled her, bouncing up and down and singing some song in their high-pitched dolphin language.

"Whoops," I said. I'd forgotten to open the game. I clicked on it now.

"This is my friend Marcus," I said. "And he brought you some fruit!"

The little Vegans squealed and ran over, quickly grabbing as much as they could from the bag and then running back to their blankets.

Vera rose and started toward us. "What happened to your shirt?" she asked, her nose hole opening and closing like she was sniffing the air.

"We found two more Vegans in the school cafeteria. One of them threw up on me."

Vera let out a little snort. "I know which one that was. He always eats too much too fast."

Marcus held out a hand. "Nice to meet you, Vera."

Vera glanced at me, almost for approval, and I nodded. Then she reached out a hand . . . and slapped his. Hand shaking must not have been a thing in their world.

"Nice to meet you, Marcus," the robotic translation said.

"You didn't tell me the Vegans were super strong," I said. "They yanked a locker door off!"

Vera tilted her square head to the side. "I did not realize you could not also do that. Strength is relative to what you know." She gazed down at the ground. "Bob is even stronger than we are."

"Well, that's a frightening little factoid," Marcus said.

The Vegans had devoured a couple oranges and tossed the apples, which were apparently the less preferred fruit, to the corner near the shelving. Now they inched closer to Marcus and his bag of wonders.

Marcus crouched down so he could be eye to eye with them. Or eye to neck. Whatever.

"Nice to meet you. I'm Marcus."

"Marcus! Marcus!" they yelled, bouncing up and down. They seemed to have unlimited energy. Must have been all that natural sugar. They grabbed the bag from Marcus's outstretched hand and emptied it out, sending fruit tumbling everywhere.

The garage door opened again behind us. We watched as Willa and Charlie came in together.

"Sorry I'm late," Willa said, unfurling her long hair from its bun. "I had dance."

Charlie glanced at Marcus. "What are you doing here?"

"He's a part of this now," I said. "I need more help." I added silently, *since you're too busy with your team all the time.*

As the little Vegans busied themselves throwing fruit in the air, I filled Vera, Charlie, and Willa in on our adventure in the cafeteria.

After I finished, I sank down to the floor, exhausted, and pulled my knees up to my chest. "We left a window unlocked so we can sneak back in tonight after dinner. The school will be empty. But even with the translator app, they won't trust us."

Charlie sat down beside me. "And we can't risk bringing Vera all through town to get her to the school."

Willa gracefully slid down into a split and then swung one leg over the other. "We need a new idea."

Marcus was in the far corner of the circle, near the pile of Grandpa Tepper's winter stuff. As he moved to sit, he slipped on an apple and went flying backward. He landed on a shovel, which sprang up in the air and knocked over a bag of driveway salt. The salt spilled across the floor of the garage, right to where Vera was seated, all three of her legs crossed daintily.

Vera's neck eyes took on a glazed look, fluttered a moment, and closed. She slumped to the side, then fell to her blanket.

I crawled over to her, panic leaching into my voice. "Vera? Vera!"

"What happened?" Marcus asked, rubbing his head as he got up from the mess.

"You killed Vera, that's what happened," Willa said.

My eyes went to Vera's chest, which rose up and down slightly. "She's not dead. She's breathing."

"But she's clearly sick." Willa pointed at Vera's still body. "Something is happening."

"Slugs," Charlie muttered.

"What?" Marcus asked.

Charlie brought his hands to his face. "Salt kills slugs."

"She's not a slug!" I shrieked.

"But that doesn't mean she can't be harmed by salt," Charlie said. "We really don't know much about her species."

"Only a little bit touched her," Marcus said, his voice trembling.

I held Vera's head in my lap and rubbed her freaky translucent skin. "Come on, Vera. Come back to us."

Vera's neck eyes fluttered and opened.

"She's awake!" Willa cried.

Vera slowly sat up and looked around. "I'm sorry, I seem to have slipped into a stupor. It happens to our species when we are exposed to sodium chloride."

"Sodium chloride," Charlie said. "Salt. So your species is allergic to it?"

"No, allergic is not the correct translation. We love it. It's a calming mineral. We use it to help us get to sleep. In fact, I opened the top of that bag and scooped some out for the little Vegans' naptime earlier."

I let out an enormously relieved breath. "So you're okay?"

"Of course!" Her mouth widened as she yawned. "I could have used a little more, actually."

Marcus stood, wiping some dirt off his jeans. "Hey, you guys. I think I figured out how we can capture the other Vegans."

17

met Charlie outside after dinner and we speed-walked to school. Willa and Marcus were going to meet us there. I'd told my parents we were going to the common to play *Alien Invasion*. It wasn't too far from the truth.

It was getting to that time of year when darkness came early. The sun had already begun to set behind the big middle school building. I wasn't afraid to catch the Vegans in the dark. They might kick my shins, but nothing more. Bob, however, could be lurking anywhere, and he was capable of anything.

Charlie pushed open the window I'd left unlocked and climbed in. Then he went to the front door and unlocked it for the rest of us. I slid inside, keeping an eye out for the others.

"So why did you bring Marcus into this?" Charlie asked out of nowhere.

I counted off on my fingers. "He's super smart. He's a great gamer. We can trust him. He helped us with the monster problem."

Charlie snorted. "Sure."

"Why are you giving me a hard time?"

"Because I want you to admit the real reason. Your *crush* on him," he said teasingly.

"*Shh!*" I warned. "They could get here any second."

"Why don't you want him to know? Maybe he likes you, too."

"Just stop, please," I interrupted. "I feel awkward enough when he's around. If he knew . . . " I shuddered at the thought.

Charlie rolled his eyes. "Fine. As always, your secret is safe with me."

"Hey, guys!" Willa called, pushing the empty double stroller.

Marcus came around the corner behind her. He'd been too far away to have heard, but that was still too close for me. I enjoyed hanging out with Marcus, and I needed his help. If he knew I liked him, he might get all weirded out and avoid me.

"All set to go alien-hunting?" I asked.

Marcus lifted the bag of salt he'd carried with him. "Armed and ready!"

"We should split up into two teams," Charlie suggested. "To cover the area of the school more quickly. Whoever finds them first, text the other team."

"That's a great idea," Marcus said. He aimed a thumb at me. "I'll go with—"

"I've got Bex!" Willa yelled. Then she grabbed my arm and pulled me down the hall.

I glanced over my shoulder and watched Marcus and Charlie head the other way. I had no clue why Willa was so enthusiastic to be my partner; but whatever. I just wanted to get this done.

"Let's check the cafeteria first," I suggested.

We pulled out our phones. I opened the *Alien*

Invasion game in case we stumbled upon the Vegans and I needed to quickly translate. Willa used the flashlight app on hers to light the way down the dark hall.

A locker that wasn't all the way closed snagged on my sweater. I had to stop and take a moment to free myself, cursing whoever left their locker open. I mean, yeah, no one left anything valuable in there overnight, but was it too much to ask to swing the dial and make sure it locked? I moved away from the wall toward the middle of the hallway to avoid any other open lockers.

I noticed Willa staring at me. "What?"

"Do you like Charlie?" she asked.

"Of course," I said, in a *duh* tone of voice. "He's my best friend."

"No, I mean *like him,* like him." She wagged her eyebrows.

"Oh!" I said. "No. Not like that."

"And he doesn't like you either?"

I suppressed a groan. Why were people always so curious about this? "No. We don't think of each other that way."

Willa wasn't the first person to ask about it, and she wouldn't be the last. People apparently found the idea of boy-and-girl best friends weird. But to Charlie and me, it was all we'd ever known. I couldn't imagine my life without him. But I also couldn't imagine kissing him. Gross. It'd be like kissing my brother if I had one.

I threw my body against the cafeteria door, and it pushed inward. Willa shined her light across the empty tables.

Raising my phone high into the air, I spoke loudly. "We're here to bring you somewhere safe. Your teacher wants you to come with us."

Nothing but silence.

"We have oranges!" Willa added.

I gave her a look, and she shrugged. "It was worth a try."

I glanced into the fridge and up at the ceiling vent they'd escaped through earlier. They definitely weren't in here now. I hoped they were still somewhere in the school, and we weren't completely wasting our time.

My phone buzzed with an incoming text.

Charlie: Any luck?

I typed back: The caf is clear. You?

Charlie: Locker room empty. Going to start checking classrooms.

Ugh. It was a school night. We couldn't stay out too late; our parents would be expecting us home.

I showed the texts to Willa. "I guess we should start checking classrooms, too."

She followed me back to the hall, and I quickly scanned the darkness for anything weirdly shaped. A scuttling sound came from farther down the corridor.

I motioned with my head. "That way."

Willa walked close by my side, like she was scared. Which was strange because Willa was so confident, I thought she'd never be afraid of anything.

"So what will it take?" she whispered.

I squinted at the air in front of us as we crept forward. "Huh?"

"For you to forgive me. What will it take?"

I glanced at her and forward again. "Really? We're

doing this now?" The mystery of why Willa had wanted to partner with me was solved. She wanted to ask me uncomfortable questions when I couldn't run away.

"I helped you with the monsters. I'm helping you with the aliens now. I apologized this summer. But when Vera asked if I was your friend, you said no. Are we enemies?"

"No," I said honestly.

"Then what are we?"

I chewed on my lower lip. "A work in progress."

Willa threw her hands up and the light from her phone bounced all around, temporarily blinding me.

"Keep it steady," I hissed. "I need to see what's in front of us."

"Why won't you just say we're friends again?"

"Because I don't trust you!" I blurted. "We were *great* friends. I was almost as close to you as I am to Charlie, but you dumped me to hang out with the popular crowd. And then you teased and bullied me any chance you could, to make sure I got the point that I wasn't good enough for you anymore. So it's kind of hard to believe that you're my old friend again. Or that you won't hurt me again. I need time.

My emotions don't go back and forth that fast. I'm a human, not a game of ping-pong."

My phone buzzed.

Charlie: We found them! Mr. Durr's classroom!

"We have to go back the other way," I said. "The boys found them."

We whirled around, ready to dash toward the classroom, but stopped short as a shadow loomed in the darkness ahead. Someone must have crept up behind us as we argued. Willa aimed her phone and the light revealed our stalker—Bob. He stood still as stone in the dim light, three legs spread wide, weird hair looking even messier than usual on top of his blue head.

I let out a shriek.

Willa jumped back, startled. Then she narrowed her eyes. "Is that alien wearing a toupee?"

Bob growled, baring his teeth like an animal. I realized I had the game open, and he'd just heard Willa's insult translated.

"Um, we mean you no harm," I said while stepping backward. Maybe he could be reasoned with.

"We're trying to help you get home, actually. Is that what you want? Do you want to go back home?"

"No," he seethed. It was strange. The translator was the same robotic voice, but it seemed more ominous coming from him.

"What *do* you want?" Willa asked, gripping my arm so tightly, I thought her fingernails would cut me.

Bob extended one long, crooked finger and aimed it at me. "I want that."

Me? Did he mean me?

"Turn the app off," Willa said.

I slid my finger over the screen of my phone. "Why?"

"So he can't understand this." She covered her mouth with her hand and whispered. "The gym is to our right. We run in there and then leave through the other doors, which lead to the B Wing."

That was a good plan. That would empty us out right near Mr. Durr's classroom.

Bob inched toward me, clicking his teeth.

"Now!" I yelled.

We darted into the gym and locked the door behind us. Bob's body slammed into the wood. Vera had said he was super strong, so we didn't hesitate. We kept running full force through the back door and into the B Wing. As I started to get tired, I pushed forward with every ounce of strength I had, which wasn't much to begin with.

Willa got to Mr. Durr's classroom before I did, and after I crossed the threshold, she closed the door and locked it. I bent over, heaving for breath.

Charlie and Marcus turned to stare at us.

"What the—" Charlie said.

"Bob's chasing us," Willa explained. I was still too out of breath to talk. "We asked him what he wanted, and he pointed at Bex."

"We've got to get this done quickly then," Charlie said. "Get down from there, right now!"

He pointed up at the fluorescent lights on the ceiling and the two little aliens who were hanging upside down like they were playing on monkey bars in a playground.

"What about the salt?" I asked.

Marcus looked unsure. "I could throw it up into the air and maybe have some of it reach them. But what if it takes effect immediately, and they fall to the ground? They could get hurt."

I glanced at the little window in the classroom door. No sign of Bob yet, but he'd find us soon. We had no time to mess around.

I reopened the game on my phone and used my best person-in-charge voice. "Listen, you two. Your teacher wants us to bring you to safety. The bad alien with all the hair is here." I used my hands to mime a big pile of hair on the top of my head.

The Vegans' neck eyes widened, and they stopped playing.

It was working! I kept going. "We have sodium chloride to help you take a nap. When you wake up, you will be with your teacher in a safe place."

Willa coughed into her hand, and I got the hint.

"We have lots of oranges there," I added.

That was enough to push them over the edge. They came swinging down and landed on the black science tables. Marcus quickly doused them in salt, and they slid down into their sweet slumber.

"I'll carry one," I said, scooping it into my arms. It weighed about the same as William Shakespaw.

Charlie grabbed the other.

"I'll get the doors," Willa offered.

We'd left the stroller at the main entrance. We

had to make it there, buckle the aliens in, and run across town to Grandpa Tepper's garage. All without Bob catching us. It seemed impossible.

"What should we do about Bob?" I asked.

"Leave that to me," Marcus said, looking angry. I'd never seen Marcus anything other than cool and chill.

Willa opened the door and checked both directions. "Seems clear."

It wouldn't be clear for long, I knew. Our heavy footsteps marched and squeaked down the hall. It was hard to be quiet on waxed floors when you were carrying unconscious aliens.

"This way," Marcus said, leading our pack.

Willa jogged beside him, lighting the way with her flashlight app. We went to the end of the B Wing and turned left into the main hall. The alien was getting heavier in my arms and I had to shift its weight. But we could see the main door. We had a clear line to it. Was it really going to be this easy?

We were almost home free when Bob came careening around the corner and blocked the door. He sneered and his lips curled back, revealing a line of short but pointy teeth.

"Oh, corn nuts," I croaked.

Willa aimed the flashlight beam directly into his eyes, which would have blinded any human and make him turn away in pain. But it didn't bother Bob. His eyes didn't even blink. In fact, they never moved away from me. Why was he staring so hard at *me*? What did he want?

His three legs bent at their knobby knees like a runner gearing up for the start of the race. Then he launched forward. But I didn't even have time to gasp before Marcus came barreling over, catching the alien by surprise and pushing him into an open locker.

Marcus swung the dial, locking him in, and then he turned to the rest of us. "He'll bust out of there soon enough, but at least this will give us a head start."

I mentally apologized for complaining about kids leaving their lockers open earlier. Totally changed my mind on that one. Open lockers were the best!

stood outside my house, waiting for Charlie in the cool morning air. My breath made puffs of white as I yawned for the fourth time. That must have been some sort of personal morning record. I was mentally and physically exhausted. My arms were sore from running around the school while carrying a sleeping alien. And my brain was foggy from not enough sleep. Constant nightmares about Bob had kept me tossing and turning. Why was he so focused on me? What did he really want?

I glanced over my shoulder at the backyard. My eyes scanned the shadows along the tree line, expecting Bob to emerge from the morning gloom any moment. But he didn't. So far, he seemed to prefer the darkness of night.

"Sorry I'm late," Charlie said, jogging up to my side. "I had a hard time getting out of bed this morning."

"Join the club," I groaned. "We should walk fast. We don't want to miss the first bell."

Jason came running outside. He put a hand up as he neared us. "I don't want to know what kept my brother up half the night. I really don't. Leave me out of it." Then he ran toward the high school.

I shrugged. It wasn't like we wanted to involve him anyway. We moved quickly, not even bothering to play our kick-the-pebble game.

Charlie shoved his hands in the pockets of his sweatshirt. "Now that we know they're looking for oranges, I have an idea about where we can search after school today for the last two Vegans. The grocery store."

I'd thought of that, too. It was the best lead we

had. If they were hunting oranges, it would make sense that they'd be there—or that they'd already been. I just hoped no one else caught them in the meantime. I wanted to send them home, not have them experimented on.

"Don't you have practice after school?" I asked.

"Not today. Coach is going to Runswick to meet with their coach about his kids' behavioral problems." He winced guiltily.

Blaming the whole thing on the Runswick Martians team was a smart idea, but we couldn't keep using it. Sooner or later, people would figure out that Runswick hadn't been pulling pranks. And then they'd start looking for the real aliens.

We reached the school with a couple of minutes to spare. The buses had come and gone, but parents were still dropping kids off and driving away.

"So we'll meet after school, then," I said. "I'll tell Willa and Marcus."

Charlie's expression changed, and he narrowed his eyes.

I crossed my arms. "I really don't want to hear any more thoughts about including Marcus."

"It's not that." Charlie pointed at something behind me. "It's here again."

I glanced over my shoulder. That same plumbing van from the other day was parked a bit down the road. "Maybe they're working at the school today?"

"Then they'd be parked in the school lot," Charlie said. "But they're not. They're down the road where there are no houses, no nothing. Just a sight line to us."

I wanted to call Charlie paranoid. I'd thought he was the other day when we saw the van twice. But a third time? Maybe something *was* going on.

Charlie squinted like he was trying to read the advertisement on the side of the van. "Have you ever heard of Meleski Plumbing?"

I thought for a moment. "No, but it's not like I keep track of all the local plumbers. If we have any problems in our house, my uncle comes over and fixes it."

The school bell trilled loudly. *Oh, no!*

"We have to go," I said, tugging the sleeve of Charlie's sweatshirt.

He came with me but kept one eye on the van

until we were inside the school and could no longer see it.

After two quizzes, one exhausting game of floor hockey in gym, a moderately gross lunch, and several lectures, during which I almost needed to prop my eyes open, the school day was over. Willa and Marcus met me in the parking lot. We were just waiting for Charlie. Which was strange because he usually walked out of school at the same time as I did.

He came a minute later, eyes scanning left and right. I knew he was looking for that van again.

"Ready to head to the grocery store?" I asked.

"Sure," he said, without as much enthusiasm as usual, like his mind was elsewhere.

Wolcott had a weird bylaw that said we couldn't have any chain stores in town. Sometimes it stank, like when you wanted a fast-food burger. But other times it was pretty cool. Like how everything was located downtown in our quaint center. A magazine had even done a feature on us once. They called Wolcott a "quintessential New England town filled with mom-and-pop stores."

And the law was convenient now because we only

had one grocery store, and it was located right in the town center near Bodhi's Diner, a short walk from school.

We reached the store in no time and started moving our way down the main row to the fruit aisle, which was, of course, the last one. We passed the breakfast cereals, the candy aisle, pasta, and more.

"This store is making me hungry," Marcus said.

My own stomach grumbled in response.

A giant "Fresh Fruits and Vegetables" sign greeted us at the last aisle. We cut past the lettuce and cucumbers and the surprising variety of tomatoes. Seriously, why was one kind of tomato so cheap and the other so expensive? Did one taste like candy? That was the only explanation that made sense to me.

We searched the bins, but couldn't find the oranges. Even the blueberries and strawberries looked picked over. Though the apples were still piled up.

"You guys," Willa said. "The oranges are gone. So either everyone in town decided they wanted them and the store sold out or—"

"The Vegans already got them all," I finished.

"Can I help you kids?"

I turned to face a short man with a mustache

that looked like a giant caterpillar. His name tag said "Bob." Thankfully he wasn't the Bob we were hiding from.

"Where are all the oranges?" Charlie asked.

Bob looked around, then leaned in toward us and whispered, "There was a robbery."

Willa fake-gasped. "And *only* oranges were taken?"

"Some other fruits, too. But *all* our oranges were wiped out. Even the extra inventory we had in the back. Strange, right?"

"Very strange," I agreed. "When did this happen?"

"Overnight," Bob said. "The place was trashed, too. Boxes tossed around, food on the ground. It was like someone had a party."

Marcus spoke up. "Were you able to see anything on security-camera footage?"

Bob shook his head sadly. "We're a small, family-owned business. It would take a chunk of change to install cameras all over the store. But we might have to do it after this wake-up call."

"Do you know anywhere else in town that sells oranges?" I asked. "My mom asked me to get some on my way home."

"The only other place is the little fruit stand

near the common, but the stand isn't always open. Good luck."

Bob wandered off, fixing an apple pyramid on his way.

Charlie stared at me. "You have that I-have-an-idea look on your face."

My stomach growled embarrassingly loudly. "I do. Let's grab something to eat and I'll explain."

"Breakfast all day at Bodhi's?" Willa suggested.

All of our grumbly stomachs heartily agreed.

Only one parking lot separated the grocery store from the diner, but Charlie lagged behind us as we walked. He was never one to dillydally when pancakes were involved. I glanced over my shoulder and watched as he furiously typed on his phone. He was so focused that he nearly tripped over a speed bump. We all stopped to wait for him to catch up.

"Charlie, come on," I said.

He narrowed his eyes at his phone as he scrolled, ignoring me.

"Hey!" Willa snapped her fingers in front of his face. "Are you with us or were you also transported to another planet?"

He looked up from the phone but not at us. His

eyes scanned the lot and the cars parked along the street.

"Are you looking for the van again?" I asked.

"Yeah," he admitted. "But it doesn't seem to be here now."

I turned to explain to Willa and Marcus. "Remember that plumbing van we saw the other day in two separate places? It was parked by the school this morning."

"Like it's following you," Marcus said. "Creepy."

"It gets worse." Charlie waved his phone. "I just did some searches and Meleski Plumbing does not exist."

"What do you mean it doesn't exist?" Willa asked.

Charlie squared his shoulders. "There is no such company. That advertisement on the side of the van is fake."

19

Vanya's mom seated us at my favorite table by the window, and we all put in our pancake orders.

I leaned forward, resting my elbows on the table and whispered. "If that plumbing company doesn't exist, then who's in the van? And why are they following us?"

Charlie fiddled with his napkin. "I don't know. But we should be careful to make sure we don't lead them to the Vegans."

It couldn't be a coincidence that a strange, fake

plumbing van had started following me right when I'd begun to shelter aliens in town. It must have been one of those government agencies Mr. Durr had talked about. They wanted the Vegans. They would keep them in cages, maybe experiment on them. Tears threatened to fill my eyes at the thought.

"Are you okay?" Willa asked, her voice soft.

I gazed down at my paper placemat. "I'm worried. What if we don't catch the Vegans in time? What if something happens?"

Marcus reached across the table and patted my hand. "We're all here together. We're going to find them."

Charlie shot up in his seat, his eyes staring at something out the window. We all watched as a slow-moving black SUV with tinted windows slid to a stop in a parking spot right outside the restaurant. My throat went dry. Were they here for me? Were they going to force me to give them the Vegans?

All the doors of the giant SUV opened and a bunch of enormous dudes piled out. My nerves went into overdrive. Then Jason climbed out of the backseat.

"Isn't that your brother?" Marcus asked.

Charlie blew out a relieved breath. "Yeah."

"He has a friend who can drive?" Willa asked.

"My brother's a freshman but he's on varsity, so he has some older friends," Charlie explained.

The little bell on the front door jangled as Jason walked in. His eyes went right to our table. He stared for a moment at our hunched over, worried looks. Then he put a hand out, stopping the crowd of guys behind him.

"Too many little kids here," he said, leading them out. "Let's go somewhere else."

"Wow," I said. "He *really* wants no part of this."

"This summer, a fire-breathing monster you released from a game nearly ate him," Willa pointed out. "Can you blame him?"

I shrugged. "I guess not."

They all piled back into the huge SUV and drove away. No plumbing van took its place. No one suspicious came into the diner. It was time to get down to business. No more distractions.

Our waitress brought our plates, filled with pancakes bigger than our faces.

Okay, I was now slightly distracted. But I could eat *and* plan.

"So," I said, chewing a bite. "We know the Vegans are hunting oranges. What if we lay a trap?"

"Like put a pile of oranges in your backyard and wait?" Charlie asked.

"Yeah." I stabbed a piece with my fork. "We buy out the fruit stand and then we're the only orange game in town."

Charlie nodded as he chewed. "There's no school tomorrow, because of that professional development day. We should be allowed to stay up late tonight. We could all wait for them together, like a stakeout."

"What if Bob shows up instead?" Willa asked.

I thought for a moment. "Then we salt him. Tie him to a tree."

"And then what?" Marcus asked.

That was the problem that had been stewing in the back of my head all day. Even if we did catch the last two Vegans *and* Bob, then what?

I shifted in my seat. "Even if we catch them all and corral them in Grandpa Tepper's garage, they can't stay there forever. I have to figure out how to send them home."

Willa pointed at my phone that lay on the table. "You brought them here somehow using the *Alien Invasion* game. Can't you use it to send them back?"

"No, I've tried that. All the game functionality just works normally."

Charlie squirted a ridiculous amount of maple syrup onto his plate. "That must mean you need that astronomer's machine. Your phone was in the middle of it when you hit Summon and brought the aliens here."

"Yeah," I said. "But if we retrace the same steps, we'll just bring *more* aliens here, not send the existing ones back."

Marcus stopped with his fork in midair. "Then what if you reverse the functionality?"

I shook my head. "I broke into the app and checked it out, but there are too many variables. I don't know what's what."

"I have a decompiler on my laptop that can turn the APK into source code," he said.

I sat up straighter. "Can you bring it tonight? If we can find the line of code that caused all of it, we could rewrite it."

Marcus's eyes twinkled with excitement. "And then recompile, install it on your phone, and *bam!*"

Charlie's forehead wrinkled. "I'm one of the smartest people I know and I have no idea what you two are saying."

"Yeah," Willa agreed. "I got the *bam* part, but that's it."

My mind churned with anticipation. This was a great plan. We would lay a trap of oranges for the Vegans and while we waited, Marcus and I could try to reverse the code in the game. But then my heart started to sink as worries crept in.

I chewed on my lower lip. "What if we can't find the right section of code to reverse? What if we're in over our heads? It would be great if we had help from people who . . . "

My voice trailed off as a thought occurred to me. I didn't know why it hadn't also occurred to Marcus. It was obvious.

"Had help from who?" Charlie asked.

I looked at Marcus. "I know you don't want to reveal their identities, but we're in deep here. I think it's worth breaking the secret. We need the Gamer Squad."

Willa nearly choked on a sip of water. "The *what?*"

Marcus's confident smile crumbled like an overdone cookie. He didn't say anything. He seemed to be involved in an intense staring contest with his plate. So I explained. "The Gamer Squad is a private, secret group of elite gamers and programmers in town. I got an invitation to join, but I refused because they weren't also inviting Charlie."

Charlie's mouth dropped open and a light blush colored his cheeks.

"Is that so?" Willa said in a strange tone, her eyes darting from Marcus to me and back again.

I ignored her weirdness. "Yeah. And Marcus didn't want to reveal the identities of the other members of the group before, but I think it's important now because we'll need all the help we can get to reverse this code."

Willa tapped her fingernails slowly on the table. "I think that's a great idea, Bex. Marcus, tell us the names of all the other people in your little secret group."

Charlie looked just as confused as I did, but the wheels were apparently turning in Willa's brain— and for some reason Marcus still wouldn't speak.

"Marcus, come on," I said, frustration leaking into my voice. "This is important. Tell us the names."

"Yeah, be honest," Willa said teasingly.

Marcus put his fork down and wiped his mouth with a napkin. Then he looked up at me. "There are no names. There is no Gamer Squad. It never existed."

20

here is no Gamer Squad," I said slowly as if sounding out the words would help me understand them. "There is no group of elite gamers. Just you and me?"

"Yes," Marcus croaked.

"Then why make a big deal out of it? Why the note and the secret meeting?"

Marcus stared down at his hands. "I wanted to hang out with you."

"And you couldn't, like, ask me to hang out? You had to create a fictional secret group of gamers?"

Marcus wouldn't meet my eyes. "Well, I thought you and I could be the first, and then we'd add more over time."

"But you wouldn't let me add Charlie." I was so confused. None of this made any sense.

Willa groaned and threw her hands up. "He likes you, blockhead!"

I blinked quickly. "What?"

"How can someone so smart be so stupid?" she muttered, shaking her head. "Marcus didn't add Charlie because he was worried that you liked Charlie, and he wanted you to spend time with him instead."

My head snapped back toward Marcus. "Is that true?"

Before I even knew what was happening, Marcus tossed some money on the table and ran out of the restaurant. Willa rolled her eyes. Charlie's jaw was practically on the floor.

I sat, stunned. Marcus liked me? My brain went numb with shock. I opened my mouth to speak but I seemed to have forgotten what words were and how to use them.

Willa elbowed me in my side. "You like him, right?"

I nodded vigorously.

"Are you really going to sit here and let him run away all embarrassed, thinking he just made a fool of himself?"

I shook my head.

She smiled. "Do you need me to come with you or do you think you'll be able to speak on your own?"

"I . . . speak," I managed. Then I started pulling money out of my pocket.

"Don't worry about it," Charlie said. "Pay me back later. Go!"

I dashed outside, looking left and right. If Marcus had been running this whole time, I'd never catch up. But I saw him walking slowly, head down, toward the gazebo in the common.

I jogged to catch up. He must have heard my ragged breathing as I got close because he turned around and stopped.

"Wait," I said, bending over to catch my breath. "Wait up."

Marcus sat down on the bottom step of the gazebo. "You don't have to say anything because you feel bad. I get it. You and Charlie forever, blah, blah, blah."

"It's not like that," I said, sitting down beside him.

"It's not?" His eyes filled with hope.

"Charlie and I are best friends and always will be. But I like someone else."

"Oh," Marcus said, his shoulders sagging. "Who?"

He really didn't know? I smirked. "He's a year older than I am and super smart. He's an awesome gamer, and I recently found out that he's really brave. Sometimes he's too sarcastic, but sometimes I'm too sarcastic, so I guess that's okay."

"Do you mean . . . ?" Marcus slowly pointed toward his chest.

"Yes, *you*, dummy."

A giant smile spread across his face. "I like you, too, dummy."

An awkward silence drew out between us. As much as this was one of the top three most exciting moments of my life—Marcus liked me! OMG!—my mind went back to tonight and everything we had to do.

I rested my elbows on my knees. "So there's really no Gamer Squad?"

"Nope."

Dread churned in my stomach. "So we're on our own tonight."

"Not quite, lovebirds," Willa said, coming around the other side of the gazebo with Charlie. "I hope you didn't forget about us."

Not for a second. Willa didn't know how to program, but she could be the lookout for the Vegans. Charlie's chemistry knowledge probably wouldn't come into play, but maybe those football tackles would. Working together as a team, we could do this.

I stood, feeling a sense of determination rising inside of me. "This ends tonight. We're going to catch the rest of the aliens, fix the code, and send them back home."

Willa aimed a thumb at the woman and her son who were setting up their fruit stand. "I'll go buy all their oranges."

"I'll bring my laptop," Marcus offered.

"We can set the trap in the small patch of woods in my backyard," I said. "And I'll bring the salt."

Charlie raised a finger into the air. "Not to burst this bubble of enthusiasm we've got going, but we have one little problem."

I raised my eyebrows. "And that is?"

"We need to replay what we did the night of the

field trip with the reversed code. But how do we get a whole bunch of aliens to the observatory?"

I thought for a minute. We would need a giant car with multiple rows of seats. Then I remembered Jason and his friend with the SUV. "I think we will need to involve someone who *really* doesn't want to be involved."

Charlie shook his head. "No. Please, no."

I gave him a look. "His friend's SUV is big enough to fit all of us and the aliens."

"How am I supposed to convince Jason to get involved?" he screeched. "And how would I explain a truck full of aliens to his friend?"

I patted him on the shoulder. "You're smart. You'll figure it out."

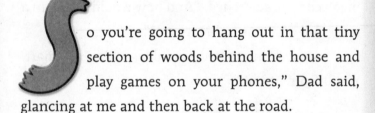

21

So you're going to hang out in that tiny section of woods behind the house and play games on your phones," Dad said, glancing at me and then back at the road.

We were on our way to my favorite pizza place to bring take-out home for dinner. Since we didn't have school tomorrow, I'd run the idea past my parents to let me stay out late with my friends, catching video game aliens.

"Yep, that's the plan," I said.

He shook his head. "Your games are very different from mine. When I was your age, I stayed in the house with my Atari."

"If I could go back in time and show your little Atari-loving self what games of the future looked like, you would be pretty psyched. You wouldn't even consider sitting on the couch and watching home-design shows with Mom."

Dad laughed, one of his big booming laughs that usually embarrassed me in public. But it was just the two of us in the car, so I didn't care. I laughed along with him.

"You make a good point, kid." He gave me a wink. "Maybe I should start downloading some of those games on my phone. Maybe I'm missing out."

I continued to smile, but on the inside I drew back. I didn't want Dad to play my games. In fact, after we got the alien problem squared away, I was deleting *Alien Invasion* and every other Veratrum game from all my devices. This made two games in a row that had unleashed chaos on my town. I wasn't taking any chances.

Dad's car slid into a parking spot. He handed me a wad of bills. "Want to run in and get the pizza?"

"Sure," I said. Anything that got us off the topic of games.

Wolcott House of Pizza was a small, dimly lit restaurant that mostly catered to people getting take-out. But they had a few tables if you didn't mind the noise and the front door constantly opening and closing while you were trying to eat. I walked up to the counter and checked on our order. It wasn't ready yet, but I paid the cashier and stepped back to wait.

A couple of Willa's popular friends—Chloe and Megan—were giggling at a table, and I didn't want them to see me. So I grabbed a seat behind a giant fake potted palm tree and scrolled through my phone.

"Order sixty-two!" the burly man behind the counter yelled.

I glanced at the receipt in my hand. I was order sixty-four, so it wouldn't be long.

The little bell rang as the door opened. Willa glided in, her long hair trailing behind her as the wind carried it. She looked like she was in a commercial for expensive shampoo. I glanced down at my reflection in the darkened screen of my phone and noted all the frizz that had escaped my ponytail. I looked like the "before" part of a commercial.

"Sixty-two," Willa said as she plopped some money down on the counter.

The man handed her a giant pizza box. I thought about getting up to say hi, but before I could, her two friends jumped up from the nearby table.

"Willa!" they called, as they hovered around her like hummingbirds, one fixing the collar of her pink shirt while the other picked off a piece of possibly imaginary lint.

"Hey, guys," Willa said. "Good to see you. My mom's waiting in the car, though."

"Will we see you tonight?" Chloe asked. "At Robbie's birthday party?"

I watched through two plastic palm fronds. Willa hesitated and got that *oh, no* look on her face you get when you realize you totally forgot about something.

"You forgot, didn't you?" Megan crossed her arms.

Willa grimaced. "Yeah, I totally did. I have other plans. I'll have to miss it. Sorry!"

She turned to leave but then Chloe practically yelled at her back, "Are you hanging out with Bex Grayson?"

Megan made a horrendous face at the mere mention of my name. "Yeah, what is with you lately? Are you turning into a nerd?"

Willa froze in place, the pizza box held out in front of her. Then she slowly turned around.

My heart rose up into my throat. I didn't want to watch this. I didn't want to hear it. But I couldn't turn away. I'd spent the last few weeks trying so hard to trust Willa after she'd thrown our friendship away like an out-of-style sweater. We were so close to becoming real friends again. And now it was all going to blow up right in front of my face. Well, not really, since I was hiding behind an artificial palm tree. But pretty much.

"Yes, I'm hanging out with Bex again tonight," Willa said. But her voice didn't show any embarrassment or fear. It was loud and confident.

She raised her chin defiantly. "And, yeah, I am kind of nerdy. It's who I am. Take it or leave it. You're my friends, but Bex is, too. I was a jerk to her for a long time, mostly to impress you. But I won't do that again. If you want to be cool with me, you have to be cool with her. We're a package deal."

The girls stood silently for one shocked moment. Then Chloe broke the silence. "Okay, fine. Relax."

Megan twisted a long strand of hair around her finger and shrugged. "We'll see you tomorrow then."

The girls walked back to their table, and Willa walked out. No big fight. No drama. No grand betrayal. My chest rose and fell as my pounding heart slowed back to normal.

"Sixty-four!" the man yelled.

I snuck around the potted tree, grabbed my pizza from the counter, and flew out the door.

Dad was singing in the car. Terribly. He turned down the radio as I slid into the passenger side.

"Hey, was that Willa I saw coming out of there a minute ago?" he asked.

"Um, yeah."

"Are you friends or not friends these days?"

I grinned to myself. "I've been pretty confused about that, but I think I've figured it out."

22

With my belly happily full of pizza, I brought a picnic blanket out to the small area of woods behind my house. The sun had almost completely set, and a couple of stars had already begun to twinkle in the clear sky.

Charlie was already there, stacking up the oranges Willa had bought from the fruit stand. "Pyramid or square?"

I chuckled. "Does it really matter?"

"Pyramid," he decided. "It looks cooler."

I shook out the blanket and laid it down beneath a nearby tree. "We are going to be staring at that pile of oranges for a long time, so anything that makes it more exciting is good."

He placed the last orange on the top. "Well, I have the most exciting job!"

I settled onto the blanket and brought my knees up. "And what's that?"

Charlie placed a rope in my hand and explained how he'd used his engineering skills to create a booby trap system that hung above the trove of oranges. My eyes followed the rope from my hand, up to a tree branch, and around the dark brown sack of salt I'd put out there earlier.

"So when the Vegans get to the pile of fruit, you let go of the rope?" I asked.

"Yep." Charlie beamed proudly at his contraption. "And the sack of salt will fall on them. Enough salt to knock them out immediately. Then you can carry one and I'll grab the other."

"Pretty cool." I nodded, impressed. "Now let's hope I can work my magic on the game's code."

Charlie sat down beside me with a *let's talk* look on his face that I knew too well. "You really refused an awesome invitation to a secret group because they wouldn't include me?"

I shrugged, feeling a little embarrassed. "Of course. You're my best friend."

"I appreciate that. But if you ever get a cool opportunity again, don't let me hold you back. We don't have to do everything together to be best friends. I mean, you're not joining the football team."

I laughed at that. "Very true."

He nudged my sneaker with his. "Are you sure you wouldn't rather hang out tonight with Marcus alone?"

I gave him a look. "Just because I have a new friend that doesn't mean I'm leaving my best one behind."

He seemed pleased with that. "The same goes to you," he said. "I know you were hoping this football thing was just a phase, but it's not. I really like it. I'm having fun."

A lump threatened to form in the back of my throat and I gulped it down. "I just don't want you to change. I like my nerdy, science geek Charlie."

"People don't have to be one thing. I can be into sports *and* science. I can be a jock and a nerd!"

I laughed so hard that I snorted. "You can start a new clique. The jock nerds."

"Hey." He gave me a wry smile. "I have a science joke for you."

"Well it's about time," I said.

"Did you hear about the blood cells that met and fell in love? It was all in vein. Get it? Vein? Vain?" He wiggled his eyebrows.

I didn't want to laugh because the joke was so ridiculously terrible, but I couldn't help it. A fit of unstoppable giggles poured out of me.

"Hey, great job being quiet," Willa said as she poked her head around a tree. "The aliens will never know we're here."

Marcus came a second later, looking all cute in jeans and a gray Wolcott zippered hoodie. "I brought my laptop."

"Sit here," Charlie said, standing up from his spot next to me. "You two will need to work together."

Marcus settled down beside me and our knees knocked together. "Sorry," he mumbled.

I flashed him a smile that I hoped didn't look as awkwardly nervous as it felt. The breeze picked up and I shivered in the cool night air. I'd been so anxious that I hadn't thought to bring a jacket.

Marcus unzipped his hoodie and wordlessly held it out to me. He had a long-sleeve T-shirt on underneath.

"Thanks," I said, slipping my arms into the warm sweatshirt.

He booted his laptop and pulled a USB cord out of his pocket. "Ready to get to work?"

"Sure. But you'll need to connect to my Wi-Fi."

"Already did. You should tell your parents that using their publicly listed phone number as their password isn't the brightest idea."

I snorted. "Nerd."

"Geek," he said back with a grin.

I giggled. "Dork."

"I'm going to throw up if you two don't stop," Willa grumbled.

Marcus and I exchanged a look and stifled our laughs. Then he cracked his knuckles and began typing. We attached my phone to his PC, and his decompiler worked its magic.

While we searched the code, Charlie and Willa came up with an early-warning system that required a lookout. Willa volunteered, since she could whistle and Charlie could not. Plus, I knew he really wanted to be the one to use his rope trap.

"There," I said pointing at a section of code. "That's the summon functionality. That's what I pressed when the phone fell into the machine and teleported the aliens."

Marcus narrowed his eyes. "All the code is written in Java except this one line."

I followed his pointing finger. "That's weird. I don't recognize that programming language at all. It's not Objective C or C++ either. I've never seen it before."

"It's almost like it's a new language entirely," Marcus said with awe in his voice.

"That's it, then. That's the line we need to reverse." My heart pounded wildly in my chest.

Charlie moved closer and looked at the screen over my shoulder. "How are you supposed to reverse the code if you don't know the language?"

I chewed on my lip. "All programming languages have fundamental concepts like variables, functions, data input."

"And this looks to be object oriented," Marcus added.

"It's a surprisingly simple line of code," I said. "So what if we just switch the variables?"

Marcus looked at me. "Change from $a = c$ to $c = a$?"

I took a deep breath. "It's the best guess I have."

"Me, too," Marcus agreed.

He made the change and then spent the next several minutes recompiling the code and reinstalling it on to my phone. Next he unplugged my phone from his PC and gingerly handed it back to me.

The phone felt like it weighed a thousand pounds in my hand. We'd done it, but we didn't know if it would work. The only way to test it was to try it, and we'd only get one shot. The pressure felt like a giant weight on my chest.

"Nothing to do now but wait," Charlie said.

Darkness had fallen over the woods. We fell into an easy quiet. It was almost relaxing with the moonlight filtering through the leaves. I leaned my back against a tree and listened to the night sounds— crickets, frogs, Willa whistling . . .

I shot up. Willa was whistling! She'd seen something!

"Everyone on alert," Charlie whispered.

Marcus and I sat still as statues. Charlie gripped the rope tightly in his hands. A breeze rustled the branches. I squinted at the shadows, wishing I had night vision. We couldn't exactly bounce a flashlight beam around. We had to stay hidden, wait, and pounce.

A twig cracked behind me. I had to force myself to stay still and not turn around.

The dim glow of the Vegans' translucent blue skin flashed between two trees on the right side of my vision. That was strange. If the Vegans were coming from the right, what was coming from behind? Goosebumps rose up and down my arms. I slowly risked a glance over my shoulder. Nothing but darkness looked back.

"Bex," Charlie whispered. "Ready?"

"Yeah, sure." I forced myself to focus on the job at hand. As soon as the salt knocked the aliens out, I had to grab one of them. "Is Jason all set?"

"Yep. Just waiting for our text," Charlie said.

The Vegans moved in closer. They were kind of cute, glowing in the night. They made sniffing noises at the air. I could tell they realized the oranges were near because they were making excited clicking noises. They reached the little clearing between the trees and gasped when they saw the orange pyramid. They must have thought they just won the fruit lottery.

A little closer, I thought, watching the intense look on Charlie's face. The trap had to be timed perfectly or the salt could miss. If the aliens ran away, they'd never fall for a trap like this again.

They stepped cautiously, their neck eyes focused on the yummy-looking fruit and not at our shadows in the distance. We stayed completely still. I even held my breath.

Finally they were in perfect position. They each grabbed an orange and began devouring it with glee. Charlie let go of the rope. It slipped through his hands and rose up the tree. The open sack of salt fell down. By the time the aliens even sensed that something was happening, it was too late. They were covered in salt.

The two little Vegans exchanged shocked looks with each other and then smiled blissfully as they slipped to the ground, sleep taking over.

"It worked!" Marcus cried.

"Woo-hoo!" Charlie yelled.

I ran over to the Vegans, mentally trying to figure out which would be the lighter one to carry. I pushed some of the oranges out of the way, made sure my phone was in my front pocket, and then leaned over to scoop one up.

I couldn't believe the whole plan worked. I'd found the line of code—hopefully fixed it—and Charlie's pulley system went without a hitch. I was grinning and feeling so happy, even the alien in my arms felt light.

"Um, Bex?" Charlie said from behind me, his voice trembling.

My smile dissolved as I slowly turned around. Bob stood between the boys and me, his muscles tensed, hands clenched into claws. Now I knew what had made the sounds behind me when the little Vegans were to the right. It was Bob stalking us.

"Do you have any more salt?" I asked Marcus from the side of my mouth.

"No. It's all on the ground there."

A raspy, threatening noise came from Bob's throat. He bared his pointy teeth, saliva dripping from his mouth. Again he seemed focused on me. But not on my face. And not on the alien in my arms either.

Realization struck me like a lightning bolt, and for the first time, I understood everything. I knew why Bob had been hanging around my property. I knew why he seemed to be focused on getting me. I knew exactly what he wanted.

And it wasn't me after all.

23

Bob's eyes were on the phone sticking out of my front pocket.

Charlie had pulled out his phone and activated the *Alien Invasion* game so they could speak. "Leave her alone!" he yelled. "You can't have Bex!"

Bob snorted. "I don't want *her*. She's a lowly human. I want her device."

"Her phone?" Marcus said in disbelief. "Why?"

"I will use it—like she did—to bring others here," Bob sneered. "I will bring all my people, and we will take over Earth!"

Oh, this was bad. Like, really, really bad. He wanted to use my phone to start an actual alien invasion. This was worse than when I'd thought he wanted to eat me for dinner. He wanted to destroy *all* of humanity.

With a roar, Marcus charged at him, but Bob saw him coming this time. Growling, Bob planted his feet—all three of them—and easily knocked Marcus to the side. Marcus hit the ground with a thud and rolled into a patch of moss.

Bob was too strong to fight when he saw the attack coming. We had to catch him by surprise. But how would we do that? He could see all of us.

And then I thought, we're not all here. Willa had whistled from her lookout position to let us know she saw something. She may have made her way back here. She could have been hiding anywhere in the darkness.

Marcus pushed himself up to his knees and was doing something on the ground by the orange pile, but I couldn't tell what.

Bob inched closer to me, hands outstretched. I gripped the little Vegan tighter in my arms. I couldn't drop it. It could hit its head or something. But I couldn't let Bob just walk up and grab my phone. I had to take a risk.

"Sorry, bud," I whispered. Then I bent to the ground, dropping the little alien from a safe height.

I tried to pop back up to my feet to protect my phone, but Bob was too fast. He whipped the phone out of my pocket with one hand and shoved me backward with the other. I flew through the air a few feet and winced as I landed on a tree root.

Bob was running now. He had my phone and a plan to take over the planet. Charlie chased him, but Bob and his three legs were too fast. Charlie would never catch up. I watched helplessly from the ground. We'd lost. Bob had gotten what he wanted. All of humanity would be destroyed.

But then Willa came soaring from behind a tree. She perfectly executed a ballet *rond de jambe* with her leg extended and tripped Bob.

The evil alien lost his grip on my phone, and it went soaring through the air. Charlie, who'd never stopped running, caught it in two outstretched hands, then tucked it under his arm like a football.

Hissing and growling like a cornered animal, Bob jumped back up to his feet, only to find himself hit square in the face by a handful of salt from Marcus. That's what he'd been doing on the ground! Scooping up as much fallen salt as he could hold in his hands. Bob's eyes rolled up and he slumped to the ground.

I scrambled back up to my feet, in shock at how quickly the situation had gone from hopeless to handled.

Willa smiled. "Now that's what I call teamwork."

I carefully placed the last alien from Grandpa Tepper's garage into the back of the SUV. Jason and Caleb, his friend with the license, inspected the inventory. I knew Charlie would think of something, but this plan was brilliant. And even though Charlie was stuck doing two weeks of Jason's chores as part of the deal, Charlie thought it would be worth the extra work.

Caleb held up a bag. "I've also got that rock salt you wanted. What's that for?"

"The less you know, the better," I said, taking the bag. True words in so many ways.

"They feel so real." Caleb poked Vera, the only alien who wasn't unconscious. Thankfully, she faked it well. Then Caleb laughed and punched Jason in the arm. "Dude, you were right. This is the prank of the century! They are so scary and real looking. Those Runswick Martians will never mess with us again. Where are you going to put all these fake aliens?"

"In the Runswick boys' locker room," Charlie said, crossing his arms and attempting to act all tough-dude-like. "We just have to stop by the observatory first."

I tapped my wrist as if I had a watch on. "We should really get going."

"Yeah, totally, dude," Caleb said and dashed to the driver's side.

Marcus and Willa had already settled into one of the rows of seats. I closed the rear door.

Jason turned to Charlie and whispered, "What are you going to say when Runswick *doesn't* get pranked?"

Charlie shoved his hands in his pockets and shrugged. "That I got caught, but I didn't roll over on anyone else. I claimed it as a solo job and took all the heat." He grinned. "But the idea for the prank will still make its way around the gossip mill. And when Runswick's pranks on us suddenly stop, it'll be because they were obviously scared of my creative retaliation. I'll be legendary. A team hero."

Jason shook his head. "Your mind is a brilliant and scary place."

We all piled into the SUV, and Caleb started the engine. He seemed to be a safe driver, following all the rules. Which was good. We did not want to get pulled over right now.

I craned my neck to look at the aliens. I didn't need anyone waking up halfway there. Especially Bob. But they slept soundly in the back. For now.

"Why are we going to the observatory first?" Caleb asked as we rolled to a stop at a red light. "Why aren't we going straight to Runswick?"

"We have to pick up some other alien-themed junk for the prank," Charlie said.

"What kind of junk?"

"Don't ask, dude," Jason muttered.

Charlie leaned forward from the back seat and his voice turned serious. "If you don't know the details, you can't be ruled an accomplice if things go bad."

"Whoa." Caleb's widened eyes were visible in the rearview mirror. "Jason, you were right. Your little bro *is* supersmart."

Charlie's face beamed with pride. He glanced at Jason, who rolled his eyes and shrugged, as if to say, *Yeah, I bragged about you. Whatever.*

I held a bag of salt on my lap and was surrounded

by unconscious aliens, but the moment still warmed my heart.

By the time we reached the observatory, though, my nerves had overtaken. I was breathing fast and my hands were shaking.

"Dr. Maria is working, right?" Charlie whispered in my ear.

"Yeah." I'd called earlier and was told that they had no public viewing tonight, but Dr. Maria was working her office hours. With the cargo we brought, she had to let us in this time.

We squished four Vegans into the double stroller. The two other little Vegans, plus Vera and Bob, barely fit into a red wagon.

"That is one crowded wagon," Caleb said with a low whistle.

"They don't need to go far," Charlie said.

Just through the parking lot, up to the telescope, and across the galaxy. No biggie.

"Should I go in, too?" Caleb asked eagerly.

Jason put a hand on his chest. "Nah, bro. We'll wait here. Remember, if they get caught, we know nothing."

We knocked on the glass door like last time. And

eventually Dr. Maria came up to answer it, like last time.

She frowned when she saw it was us. She opened the door a crack. "You know I can't let you in. We've talked about this."

Charlie, Willa, Marcus, and I had been standing like guards in front of the stroller and wagon full of aliens. Now, we broke apart and watched as Dr. Maria took it all in.

I laid out my case. "I have six sleeping alien-kids, one unconscious evil alien, one conscious nice one, and a working translator. You can ask whatever you like for a few minutes if we get to use your machine."

Vera sat up in the wagon and waved.

Dr. Maria's eyes widened to the size of moons. Then she nodded fervently, apparently unable to speak as she opened the door wide.

"Can we take the elevator up to the observation level?" I asked, pulling the wagon.

Dr. Maria nodded again, pressing the button for the elevator and holding the door while we loaded it up with ourselves, the wagon, and the double stroller.

After a short ride up, we piled out. I almost gasped at the telescope, even though I'd already seen it during the field trip. It was just so impressive. The dome was open as it had been then, the clear night sky twinkling with billions of white lights.

"We need the telescope focused on Vega," Charlie said, getting right down to business.

"Is that, um, is that where they're from?" Dr. Maria asked, finally finding her voice.

"A planet orbiting Vega, yes." I pointed at the machine my phone had fallen into. "Have you made any changes to your device?"

She shook her head. "No. I haven't had the chance to work on it this week."

I blew out a breath. "Good. We need everything to be the same as it was the night our class was here."

As Dr. Maria pointed the telescope at the required coordinates, I briefly told her what had happened, from my game accidentally summoning aliens to town, to Bob trying to steal my phone to take over the world.

"And you think reversing the code will teleport them back?" she asked.

"That's our hope," Marcus said.

"Well, it's ready." She stepped back from the telescope. "May I have a few moments like you promised?"

"Of course," I said.

The game had already been open on my phone, so Vera had understood everything. She climbed out of the wagon and held out her hand to Dr. Maria. "Hello."

Dr. Maria's trembling hand reached out and shook hers. Her mouth formed a giant O as she stared at Vera in awe.

"We only have a couple minutes," Willa reminded her.

Dr. Maria nodded. "Wh-what is the secret to space travel?" she stammered.

"We do not yet know," Vera's robotic translator said. "The child's device teleported us here unexpectedly. Our current space program cannot teleport or reach the speed of light."

"Have you been watching us from afar?" Dr. Maria asked with a catch in her voice.

"We've been looking," Vera said. "We were at our own observatory when we were brought here. But we didn't know that Earth had life-forms. In our world, you are referred to as Planet Blue 436F. We have never made contact with life-forms from another planet. Until now, that is."

Dr. Maria blinked back tears as she whispered almost to herself, "They'll never believe me."

I moved close to her and put my hand on her arm. "That's okay. At least you know now that it's true. We're not alone. Your work, your machine . . . it's worth it."

"But now," Vera said, "we really need to get home."

I stared at Vera. When I first saw that upside down face, it was straight out of a nightmare. But now, I loved it.

My voice cracked. "I'll miss you, Vera."

"I'll miss you, too, my friend Bex." She looked at us, one by one. "And your friend Charlie. And your friend Marcus. And . . . Willa."

I coughed into my hand. "Actually, Willa is my friend, too."

Willa's face brightened, and I even thought I saw a single tear in the corner of her eye.

"And your friend Willa," Vera amended.

The little Vegans started to stir, which meant Bob wouldn't be too far behind.

"We need to do it," Charlie said. "Now."

I gently placed my phone in the middle of all the wires in Dr. Maria's machine where it had landed the night of the field trip. The game was open and ready to go. I glanced around—at Vera, the little Vegans, even Bob, and felt a hard lump in my throat.

"Good-bye," I said, and pressed the Summon button.

I stepped back, away from the aliens, and toward my friends. All I could do now was hope the code rewrite worked. Marcus grabbed my hand, Charlie grabbed the other, and Willa rested her chin on my shoulder.

I closed my eyes and held my breath.

24

et him!" I yelled. "Knock him down! Knock him down, hard!"

"Wow, you've *really* gotten into this," Willa said.

I rubbed my hands together. We'd crossed into October, and a chill was in the air. And on my butt. Someone should really engineer a way to heat metal bleachers for spectators.

"At first I thought football was boring," I admitted. "But it's a lot more exciting when your best friend is on the team." Even if he spent most of his time on the bench, having Charlie on the team and finally understanding what that meant to him had given me a sudden case of school spirit.

The bleacher shuddered as Marcus plopped down next to me. He handed me a hot cocoa. "Figured you could use this."

I smiled gratefully. "Thanks!"

It had been only a few days since we'd successfully sent all the aliens back to their home planet, and I still felt a little pang when I thought about Vera. I hoped she and the younger Vegans were doing well back home. And I hoped Bob was in some sort of alien jail, charged with attempted intergalactic warfare.

When we'd left the observatory empty-handed, Jason feigned shock at our getting "caught" with fake aliens. Caleb was truly disappointed. He'd wanted to drive us to Runswick's school and be a part of the best prank of all time. But, as predicted, Charlie had been treated like a hero for even thinking about such a cool prank. And, also as predicted, Runswick never retaliated. No one needed to know that they'd never started the prank war to begin with, and that those fake aliens were real.

We got our unnecessary revenge on the field.

With one second on the clock, our kicker sailed the ball through the yellow-posty things, and everyone jumped up and down screaming, so I knew we'd won. Now that I'd stopped playing *Alien Invasion*, I had extra time on my hands. Maybe I'd learn some football terms so I could understand what was going on in these games.

The three of us waited for Charlie outside the locker room. He came out, beaming from the team's win (which he had no hand in, but whatever, go team).

"Thanks for coming!" he said, his face all red and sweaty.

Marcus patted him on the shoulder. "Awesome game."

"Totally," Willa said, flinging her hair in the way that she did when a cute guy was around.

It was really starting to seem like Willa liked Charlie. And I didn't quite know how I felt about that. But, first things first. "Do you guys want to do something?" I asked.

"Sure!" Charlie said. "And, actually, I have an idea."

"Hey, Willa!" Megan yelled as she and Chloe

walked by. "We're heading to the mall. Want to come?"

"I can't," Willa called back. "Let's do something tomorrow, though!"

"Deal!" Chloe yelled.

I couldn't stop myself from grinning ear to ear.

"What?" Willa rolled her eyes playfully. "You're more exciting to hang with lately. It's not a big deal."

"What's your idea?" Marcus asked Charlie.

Charlie said, "Let's hop in my dad's car. He'll give us a ride."

I had no idea what Charlie had in mind. His dad drove us through the center of town and to the outskirts where a few industrial and office buildings stood. But when he took a right into a large lot, and a familiar red-brick building came into view, I understood. I just didn't know why.

Mr. Tepper put the car in park. "I'm going to head to the grocery store. I'll pick you up when I'm done."

The four of us got out of the car and walked toward the chain-link fence that surrounded the headquarters of Veratrum Games. We weren't the only ones there either. A small group of kids and adults stood around, like they were waiting for something.

"Charlie," I said with a tinge of anxiety. "Why are we here?"

His voice turned serious. "It's the unveiling."

"Oh!" Marcus said, excited. But then he added, sadly, "Oh."

"Anyone want to fill me in?" Willa asked.

I explained, "Whenever Veratrum announces a new game online, they always announce it here in town a few hours earlier by unfurling a banner on their building."

She pointed. "So that's why that one's being pulled off?"

We all looked. Sure enough, two men on the roof were pulling off the old *Alien Invasion* banner, which had replaced the previous *Monsters Unleashed* banner. I wondered what would be next. That old excitement started to bubble up inside me, but I shut it down. No matter how cool the game sounded, I could never play it. We could never trust a Veratrum game again.

"We all have to promise never to play it," I said. "We're just here to see what it is."

But before anyone else could agree, Charlie shot

to attention, his focus fixed on something in the employee lot. He raised an arm and slowly pointed. "Look."

I followed his line of sight. Willa and Marcus must have found it at the same time as I did because they simultaneously gasped.

The Meleski Plumbing van that had been following us was in the Veratrum Games employee parking lot.

"Well," Charlie said, "the good news is that a secret government agency hasn't been following us."

"The bad news is that my favorite video game company has," I said, pretending to be calm.

Marcus shook his head in disbelief. "Since when do game developers stalk people in fake plumbing vans?"

Willa snorted. "Since when do video game monsters escape into the real world and real aliens teleport to Earth through an app?"

"Point taken," Marcus said.

Charlie puffed out his chest. "Bex is right. We have to agree, no more messing around with Veratrum Games. Never play it. Never download it. Never open it. Not once."

"Shall we make a pact?" Willa asked.

"Hands in," I said.

We all held our arms out and placed our hands on top of one another's. Then we each solemnly swore with the words, "I promise."

I looked around at the four of us banding together and felt a warmth spread through my chest. We'd been through so much in such a short time. I felt like I could truly trust them. I had found my people.

"Hey," Marcus said with a little smile. "I guess there is a Gamer Squad after all. It's us."

The small crowd of people leaning against the chain-link fence roared and clapped. They must have unfurled the new banner. I took a deep breath and turned around to see what the next game would be. The sign read:

Get ready for Veratrum's newest augmented reality game. . . .

ZOMBIE TOWN

Charlie and I looked at each other uncertainly. *Gulp.*

Acknowledgments

I could not have written this book without a little help. Thanks to:

My agent, Kate Testerman, and my editor, Christina Pulles, for being on my squad.

Dr. Maria Womack, astrophysicist extraordinaire, for helping me with my astronomy questions and for being a good friend.

The Clay Center Observatory, for having public telescope nights when I could research this book.

Anna Staniszewski, for connecting me with Ray Brierly, who so generously answered all my programming questions.

Mike, Ryan, my parents, and all of my family and friends, for supporting me, making me laugh, and not minding that I'm a total dork.

he first sign that something was wrong was Robbie Martinez projectile-vomiting in science class. We were learning about viruses. And though I didn't think it was barf-worthy, we all have our own threshold for gross. Apparently Robbie's was thinking about a virus invading and reproducing in previously healthy cells. Or so I thought. But when Isaac made the liquid scream in math when we were only talking about ratios, I started to wonder if something else was going on.

"Hey, Bex." My best friend and neighbor, Charlie Tepper, came up to me in the hall with a concerned look. "Why is everyone eating backward today?"

I struggled to pull a book from the pile in my locker without making the rest of them come tumbling out, too. "Must be some kind of stomach bug."

Charlie grimaced. "I remember last year in Runswick a norovirus went around and half their school got it. That's how contagious it can be. They had to close the school for a week and bring in a cleaning crew."

"Gross." I closed my locker door and turned around. My friend Willa Tanaka staggered up to us, clutching her stomach.

"Willa!" I cried. "Are you sick, too?"

She shook her head, and her long black hair flowed from side to side as in one of those slow motion commercials. "I don't have whatever this illness is. But I just watched Mr. Durr upchuck a week's worth of groceries on the whiteboard. So that made me a little woozy."

Yikes. This flu was tearing through school fast. I really didn't want to stick around and risk catching it, but I couldn't just walk out. Maybe I could call my parents and ask them to get me released.

"Bex," a voice called from behind me. "Bex!"

I turned around to see Marcus Moore waving at me from the doorway to the computer lab. My heart sped up. Marcus was the fourth in our little group—Charlie, Willa, Marcus, and I made up the Gamer Squad. Self-titled, but still totally cool. We'd saved the town from video game monsters over summer vacation and an accidental alien invasion in September. My phone was responsible for both disasters, and I still felt a little guilty about that. But it had been a month without drama, and things seemed okay. Mostly because we'd agreed never to play mobile games from Veratrum Games ever again since they'd developed both games that had gone so wrong. In fact, if Veratrum's latest game were called *Flu City* instead of *Zombie Town*, I would have wondered if they were involved with the puke-a-palooza going on right now.

Even though Marcus was one year older, he and I had a lot in common. We were awesome gamers; we both wanted to be programmers; and we both agreed that Speedy's Pizza was far superior to the Wolcott House of Pizza, which was an unpopular opinion in town.

I'd had a crush on Marcus forever. Back in September, my dream came true when he told me he liked me. But now it was October, and we'd never really talked about it since. I'd been hoping that he'd ask me to the Halloween Dance, but he hadn't. At this point, it was only a week away; so my high hopes were currently somewhere in my shoes.

"Bex, c'mere!" Marcus waved excitedly.

Willa poked me in my side. "Go see your lover boy."

Charlie tried to cover a chuckle with his hand.

I rolled my eyes at both of them.

The four of us had been spending a ton of time together since the Gamer Squad formed last month. We hung out in school, played games after school, and talked all night on a group chat. Charlie had been my best friend forever. Willa and I were friends when we were little, then not friends when she dumped me for the popular crowd, then friends again. Now we were closer than ever. And Marcus, . . . well . . .

My stomach did a little *flip-flop* as I walked toward

the computer lab. Was this it? Was Marcus finally asking me to the dance?

I reached the doorway to the lab and put on my best nonchalant totally-not-expecting-you-to-ask-me-to-the-dance-and-I'm-actually-really-chill-right-now-and-not-nervous-at-all fake voice. "Hey, Marcus. What's up?"

He motioned for me to come into the room. "I want to show you a game I made."

My heart sank. A computer game? I'd gotten my hopes up—again—and he'd only wanted to talk about games—again. I mean, gaming was my favorite hobby and would hopefully one day be part of my career, but a girl wanted to be asked to a dance now and then, too!

I glanced at the wall clock. "Okay, but I only have three minutes before my next class."

Marcus was beaming with pride, but his fingers were trembling a little. Why was he nervous for me to see his game? Was he worried I wouldn't like it? He led me to the closest computer terminal. His hand hovered over the keyboard.

"Are you ready?" he asked with a giant smile.

As I opened my mouth to say yes, the intercom

clicked on and our principal, Mr. James, began to speak.

"The school is releasing early today due to the—" He paused to let out a moderately gross burp. "Due to the illness affecting many students and staff."

His voice sounded weird. As he tried to begin his next sentence, he gagged and gurgled. I knew what was coming next, but thankfully the intercom clicked off before we all had to listen to it.

Marcus's smile fell.

"That's okay," I said. "You can show me the game tomorrow."

"Sure," he said, nodding, but the disappointment didn't leave his eyes. Whatever this game was, it seemed really important to him.

Charlie poked his head into the room. "Did you hear? Mr. James is letting us out early. My mom already got the emergency autocall and texted that she'll pick us up."

"Okay, cool," I said, reentering the hallway.

With school canceled, kids were rushing out at record speeds but without the usual glee that came along with the early dismissal of a snowstorm or holiday. They were either sick themselves or trying desperately to leave without touching anything or anyone. And as Andy Badger recycled his lunch on the floor in front of me in a colorful display, only one question went through my head: Why did this have to happen on Taco Tuesday?

The next day, I would have many more questions.